Rose Diary
Short Stories

BIN SOBCHUK

ROSE DIARY SHORT STORIES

iUniverse books may be ordered through booksellers or by contacting:

iUniverse
1663 Liberty Drive
Bloomington, IN 47403
www.iuniverse.com
844-349-9409

ISBN: 978-1-6632-1672-4 (sc)
ISBN: 978-1-6632-1673-1 (e)

Library of Congress Control Number: 2021900506

Print information available on the last page.

iUniverse rev. date: 01/15/2021

Contents

1

Rose

Rose is a sex worker in Bloor West Village. Almost every night, she stands in the chain store "7/11". People called her Rose because she has a tattoo of a red rose with two leaves on her left side forearm. She is a blondie so her skin is very white. The rose tattoo is shiny and beautiful. Every night she holds a Red Bull energy drink in her left hand and waits for customers. She is used to it.

Bob is a police officer at Police 11 Division. He and his partner are in charge of this area today. It is already 1:00 am, they stop the car and walk in the 7/11 store.

Bob is watching Rose, when they come in. Rose does not withdraw and hands him the Red Bull drink. Bob lifts up his arm and looks at his watch. Rose's face turns red. Bob bought a hot dog and then they go. Bob does not forget the girl who he just met. He already notices her tattoo and her body. She is beautiful. "I should help her next time."

Police officers can choose 5 different shifts to work. Since Bob encountered that girl, he only chooses the midnight shift to work. Soon he met her in the same place again. This time Rose is shy. She just stands there and lowers her head to avoid eye contact with Bob. Bob walks up to her, pulls out the notebook, then he asks her some questions and writes down the information. He feels happy and proud to be a policeman. The third time they see each other; Bob chats with her. He persuades her to change her way of life. She did not say anything, but she has too many barriers to make a living. Since they are friends now, Bob often protects her. After work, he dates her. He drives his car with her. She is very excited. She shows her tattoo "rose" to him and brings him to her home to make love. Her skills for making love are wonderful. She is a pussy Cat! Bob's cock is red, and just like a bull's horn. Bob never made love before. He falls in love with her. She did not say marriage, because she never forgot she is a prostitute. Once she asked him to let her sit beside him in the police car. He refused. He also said I do not want you to sit in the back seat; since it is not lucky. For a long time since they met, Rose tries to go to the Police Academy to study and become a real police officer. But she is afraid of a background check. The most time, Rose is not sure how long she can have this relationship with Bob. Actually, keeping this relationship is decided by Bob.

Recently, Bob is surprised. Where is she? She is not in the store anymore and also did not call him anymore. He goes to her home. Rose's face is swollen and there are a lot of bruises on her body. Bob is furious. He asked who did it. Rose does not answer. Finally, she told him that the mafia did it. The reason why they did so, is because she has a police boyfriend! She begs Bob not to take revenge on them just for her. The mafia have many friends and are fierce. Bob thought that if he goes to their place at night; it is no different than committing suicide. He should go in the daytime.

One week passed. He and his colleague who is his best friend decided to mafia's den. They beat them, and get heroin and cash. They come back to the Division. The 11 Division police inspector praises them. After work, Bob drives his car going home. A car from behind speeds up and catches up to him. The mafia yells to Bob "Rose is my property; stay away from her!" then they shot Bob. Bob lays on the seat and drives as fast as he can. Because police have a rule that the weapons cannot be brought home, he does not have guns now. He can hear that the bullets flying towards him and his car was shot several times by the mafia. Bob flees this time. He thinks a lot. He is a man especially a policeman. Rose is a girl and bullied by the mafia and often her customers. He could not let her go away. He is afraid for her safety and for making a living. If he does not help her who will do it? He definitely cannot trust black hands to help Rose. He decides no matter what happens, he will protect her for good.

Two months passed. The Police inspector received the notice from police sex department. It shows evidence that Bob has a girlfriend and he met his girlfriend when he works … The Police inspector did not say who did it in the morning report, yet he indicates that this behavior is unacceptable. Bob and some police officers all know who.

Bob knows it is time to say goodbye to Rose. He does not want to lose his job. He also cannot marry her. Yet he still wants to protect her in secret. He finds her and tell her why he comes. She does not cry. In her mind she already knows that one day it will happen. He holds her tightly and kisses her rose tattoo. He gives her 2000 dollars but she refuses. He promised that if she calls him, he will answer the phone.

From that day, Rose is not that Rose. She disappeared from the store 7/11. She finds a regular job selling clothes. Her good behavior and beauty make her a popular sales lady too.

2

King of Gems

Roncesvalles is a traditional Polish Village in Toronto for centuries. Most Polish children are born here and grow up here and marry here. Natalie is one of them. She is a poor girl. Not only is her mother mean but she abuses her often. She is very shy and speechless. Natalie is a beautiful name that her father gave her. He blessed her in the future. She seldom goes to the parties because she always thinks that she is not perfect. Yet she loves a boy who is her neighbour; his name is Oliwier.

As time goes on, she feels that it is time to show her love to him. But how and if he refused her… Her nature is against her to do so and tortures her so long. "I am not good at words; I even do not have confidence to talk to him. He is so popular. She knows that diamonds are a girl's best friend. Coincidently, Oliwier was born in April; Diamond is his birthstone too. She has a big decision to buy a Claddagh ring with a little diamond as pure as a dewdrop water as his birthday gift. She spent all her money and bought him a diamond ring. At his birthday party, she is silent. Everybody said "Happy 21st Birthday" to Oliwier and gave gifts to him. He smiled. At last Natalie showed her diamond ring to him, he was shocked! Everyone in the party was shocked. Oliwier grew up with Natalie and knew her well. How her parents treated was something he could not forget. He knew that if he refused her and let her go, she would die! But marriage? I am just twenty one years old and I may find a better one… "I cannot let her go! I am a man." He kneeled down; one hand holding the ring and asked "Will you marry me?" She said "Yes!" He put the ring on his finger. Another big surprise for all the people. "No engagement rings just this ring for a wedding ring, I will buy a

5

ring for Natalie's wedding." Natalie cries. She saw jealous and contempt but she got her true love. That year she was 20.

Time passed fast. Now seven years had passed. He finished school and just has a small job. She works at a factory and cleans home every day. Oliwier's relatives always blames this on Natalie. This wedding is totally wrong! They should divorce.… Natalie still is speechless and tolerances all the reality. Her only true love in her mind is that he is just like a Prince, a sun in her heart. Oliwier did not knew what he should do either. He is not that young anymore and he did not feel that he is a man either, too tiny and too disappointed. They did not have child. She is shy.

Their friends began to get engaged and married. Some even have engagement diamond rings and wedding rings. Natalie and Oliwier are humiliated. Natalie works hard every day to make her husband happy. Oliwier feels guilty for being poor. But he could not forget that he is a king in his wife's heart.

3

Halloween

This is the first Halloween that I did not spend with my beloved husband. He passed away but he did not disappear. Now my money is tight, I did not buy discount candies for kids. One Chinese woman even laughed at me for that!

At evening, I turned out the light and watched TV Murdoch mysteries and the news. Suddenly, I remembered my first book's royalty still did not pay. I called the company and they still let me wait. Actually, I already feel satisfied since over 50 websites introduced my book including Indigo. There is a Norwegian website and a Japanese website.

Last night, just like every night, I cried in bed. I missed my dear late husband. Finally, I turned on the computer to watch the spanking movies. I did not do it for a while. I promised my ward Bishopric that I will not do it again. After almost one and a half hours, I stopped. I was crying because my late husband did whip me for our desire. 11 pm, I could not sleep and turned on the computer again. And watched the spanking movies. Then slept.

On Halloween I seemed to forget it during the daytime. At 7:15 pm Mervyn called me that he was coming, because he cannot come here on Wednesday as usual. I said welcome. I turned on the front room light and waited for him. Somebody knocked on the door! I opened my door. "Trick-treat" kids! Thank God! I still have some sesame candies. I gave them to two kids. "Dong dong" I opened the door to another two kids! I just have two sesame candies left. I gave to them. I began to panic. How can I answer the next knocking? If I do not answer when Mervyn comes what shall I know? I looked at my home. I found that my late husband left some candies in the jar. I have no choice and opened the jar grabbing some in my hand. I gave kids old candies. Now I could feel kids like candies just like I like being whipped-none stop. Finally, Mervyn came. He suggested that I turn off the light and we went to kitchen turned on the lights to talk. He is my mentor. I felt that I am just like his kid. I love him too. He checked my husband's mail and wrote down letters for my lawyer. Then he rushed to go.

Now I cannot say that I want him to teach me more. He did. I am stupid and saw the online movies. I am horny yet I also cannot forget the church's discipline. I am on the church's probation therefor I had oral sex with a man and he whipped me too.

I miss my late husband and I want to seal with him in the temple. But sometimes I can only cry. Love one and cannot forget. His big sense of humor and never making love with me make me ignite and purified. He made my dream happen-I published my Debut. If not for him, I may be homeless and in the hospital now! No kidding! I came to Canada fourteen years ago; I ended up in the hospitals 16 times. The night is late, I will go to bed and immerse recalling in our best time.

4

Halloween Prince

My kitty is a pure black cat called Prince. He sometimes scares the neighbours. I like a black cat especially Prince! In the morning, I changed the kitty litter boxes. I fed him salmon and tuna canned food. He likes it very much. His favorite food is cat cookies. I gave him cat cookies once, yet he wanted more. I cannot refuse him since Halloween, I gave him more cookies. He seemed satisfied.

At night he always accompanies me to sleep. He is nimble. I seldom catch him but occasionally, I pat him.

 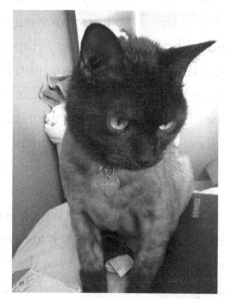

Trick or Treat

With kids "trick-treat", I give candies to them and say "Happy Halloween!" one of my neighbours hold their three months old son and lead three years old daughter to join the Halloween group. Many monsters, angles, princes, princesses, devils show.

Halloween Prince 2

Another Halloween comes. Prince did not see me for over 9 1/2 months. I was in the in hospital at that time. My neighbour went to my home to feed him for seven months then he was sent to a cat luxury hotel until I went home. He got anxious and always licked his belly. His belly has two fur free places. I bring him to the vet. My vet teaches me many methods to help my cat –Prince.

Time flies. Now it is Halloween again. My handsome black fur ball is useful. Just like usual, in the daytime he and I sleep until 12:00 pm; I wake up and clean his kitty litters. I feed him for weight control cat chow, since he is overweight two pounds. I know that it is very impolite to talk about Prince's privacy in public. I prepare the candy for kids tonight. Prince always wants to help so he pushes some candy on the table to my bag. He is excited. I can tell. At 5:00 pm, I open my house outdoor light to wait for my adorable visitors. Soon he and I stand on our veranda to welcome our Halloween "ghosts". Kids are smart and cute. While at trick-treat, I became a candy giver. Some kids are excited to see my Prince. They like to pat him, yet Prince avoids them. He knows that he is noble and untouchable. I like to give them "smarties" candy which is made by Nestle Company. I wish they would be the best generation ever. Kids are active. In the meantime almost every home turns on their outside lights or decorate to welcome them. My black Prince is my special gift to all of us. Now the weather is cold. His winter coat shines plus his beautiful collar shows his king's qualities. I love him forever. Happy Halloween!

5

David Lawson

David Lawson is a computer teacher who is in charge of two community computer centres. Today he is not happy because his student, I, did not show up on time. He is looking at the glass door and putting his two hands in his jean's back pockets. He knew that this is the first time I missed classes, but who knows? Maybe soon I will have missed a second one.

I rushed into the class and said, "I am sorry I am late" to David. The class began. David clearly and slowly explained the knowledge, yet obviously I could not focus on the class and missed the points. David noticed it and was worried. He put his hands on the computer table's both ends, and his butt slightly up. My face immediately red. I am conscious that this is my mistake.

After class, David talked to me. And he offered me a drink across the road at Tim Hortons. I said to David that my mother was sick for many years and stays at home. I sometimes take care of her. My two brothers never help my family and my father supports the family. Today, I took care of my mom and was late. I promised that I will not be late anymore. David always has some special feeling for me. Today he knew me down to earth. He sincerely wanted to drive me to his home. I hesitated. In the meantime, I know that David also recommends students to Brock University. I had missed one chance to go to university. Now it is an adult high school and I am over eighteen years old. I agreed with him.

David lives in a condo. He thought that if I can go to university to study and graduate and he and I can work together and marry. Anyway he cannot control himself either. He makes love with me; I am a virgin! He felt very satisfied.

After a semester of computer class, I went to Brock University to study. I worked hard. On the third year, I felt very tired, too much homework, projects and tests. I am exhausted. I thought about David for a long time. How about letting him help me to graduate. But if he just loves my body and… I cannot care about too much.

I came back to see David. David said that if you knew my name, you should not come back like that.

Many years passed. I still remember this failure. All though, I did not complete my university studies, I miss and thank David too. He gave me this great opportunity to pursue my academic career and he really loved me and cared about me. His favor ignites my new hopes for my whole life. I must repent that I should not go to his home that night. I need to control myself. He is the person who gives me knowledge and discipline. I also should have my bottom line. I love him; yet I cannot pursue his love anymore. He is forever my mentor.

Now I am still a single. I struggle in some low paid job. I often recall my school life. How wonderful it was! I wish that I could find another way to feed my desire to study at school again. I will not make this kind of mistake anymore. For this aim, I chose to study at Toronto Adult High School to improve my professional skills and English level. I feel that I find my happiness and confidence back. I long for a bright future, which can lead me to a new successful life. I think about this for a long long time. I have no children; partly because of the past experiences and my financial situation. I must say that I am not young anymore, but in the meantime, I became wiser. I am not that young adult student who hooked up with my teacher. I know that I was so wrong. Study is hard work. I should not try to find a short way to break the rules of our school. I want to be a good student, I should study hard and wisely. Life is short and colourful, I need to concentrate on my goals to achieve them one by one. My mother passed away three years ago. I do not need to take care of her again. For me, life is simple now. School and home are my two places to go. I had a dream to be a professional writer. My own history and knowledge become my future writing material. Here teachers are nice. I learnt plentiful new things. I hope that I could accomplish my studies soon.

6

Pure White Pleasure

Today is Lisa's computer class. Cody Cita is her new teacher. Different from David, he is a university student, so he is young. Yet it does not mean that he works hard and is qualified. The first day, Cody did not show up. This is their second time. He comes 10 minutes early. Lisa always comes earlier than the others. Class begins. Cody is polite but not helpful; Lisa listened carefully but there is no improvement. She felt strange. She did not have too many choices. It is free and one-on-one teaching. Soon one hour passed. Cody shake hands with Lisa and rushed to go. Lisa went home.

The next class will be next Monday. She felt something is wrong with Cody. Curiously, she went online and finds that Kita is a Japanese Surname, which means to come and arrive. Lisa is Chinese. It may be the reason? She did remember that he has blue eyes but not fair hair. Lisa opened the email box. Cody sent an email to her but not too pleasant.

Another Monday is coming. Lisa came and waited for Cody. He arrived 20 minutes earlier. Then they began the class. This time Cody is more useless and very sleepy. She noticed that he has a running nose, when he sneezed, there is a little bit of blood on the tissue. He kept the good temper. To be surprised, he asked Lisa many times how she can make a living. Lisa is simple and told him that she owns stocks. On the first class, Lisa tried to let Cody teach her how to transfer money online. Yet now she changed her mind. She cannot trust him anymore. It looks like Cody is a Cocaine addict. His beautiful blue eyes veiled greedy. Time passed quickly; he showed no interest in this class. He keeps saying, "You knew enough for your work. I think that you knew it …" Lisa is really disappointed. She even cannot ask questions; since he did not teach her very much. Time wasted and Cody happily went out.

On the way home, Lisa is very sad. She recalled her first computer teacher. He was strict and lovely. She wish that one day they could see each other again.

7

Face the Wall

Eleven years ago, I went to the Jesus Christ of Latter day Saints Toronto Ward. I experienced a hard time; no husband, no money. I sometimes saw pornography. I also wrote some stories. Once our bishop criticized me, "If you cannot sleep, face the wall!" I felt very shameful.

Now my husband has just passed away. I could not stop seeing online spanking movies. My husband and I did not make love during our marriage. Yet we did play whipping many, many times. He was dominant, so I was submissive. Both of us were satisfied by this style. When I bared the butt and faced the wall, I knew that he looked at my body.

I read a book of Sigmund Freud. I saw that he whipped his cleverest patient--a Russian girl "in order to attain a certain state of happiness, purity, wisdom, perfection or immortality." (Quote Reading, Writing, And the Whip) my favorite style is still whipping. I did not experience other styles, besides the belt. His whipping was just like "iron rod", a forbidden fruit in the tree of knowledge of the Garden of Eden. I desire it and taste it and obsess about. God really punishes me at any second. I cannot get rid of it so far. I am a losing lamb and do not know the right way to come back and to be normal. I even did not know that I should be punished or if I already have been. I wrote vividly and gave my book to the bishop but he did nothing to me and put my book in his office. I knew he is busy and I am so tiny.

Now I am very lonely and dangerous; since my husband passed away. I held the pillow to sleep just like holding him. I face the wall to sleep and try to forget our secrets. Nothing works. I need a leader who can teach me how to get out of this dilemma. Church leaders are my first choice. I am afraid that my psychiatrist will become the second Freud and I will sacrifice my body and time to a wrong way. My beloved husband could deliver strokes but it did not mean everybody can do it. I still had my bottom line.

Please help me and give me the right lead. No matter what I will accept it. Thank you.

8

Night

Night, it is my self-education time. I study in school in the daytime. I dreamed my future to be a superman! Yet reality often laughs at me. I am not one of the school ball games members; I even abuse myself for missing gym classes. The reality fights back. I wear eyeglasses now.

Soon, I graduated from university. Tons of resumes I sent are as silent as falling to the sea's floor. Fortunately, Walmart did reply to my resume. My career is to be an accountant, yet they said no. I am anxious and want a job. They accept me as a casher. 5.5 feet is my height. With eyeglasses, I am a clown now! I have another dream. A cool hair cut can win some shots. I keep fashion first and wait for my promotion and my girl. Yet it is not.

The cashier's job is very easy for many of us. I could not forget my university's knowledge. That is my capital. I asked our manager to change my job to a night time clerk. He agreed to it. I cannot forget how many times my eyeglasses are covered with frost when I come in or out the cool storages. I count the goods' day in and day out. I learned the information from the morning and evening meetings. One day, I finished my project. I gave it to my manager. He was very surprised and encouraged me. I got the promotion. I was not just a night time clerk. I become an assistant accountant! I knew that my real career had begun at Walmart. It is true. Also I still keep my cool hair; I believe that my girl is not far from me now!

9

To God's Messenger

I am pretty happy today. Many people in different positions teach me the meaning of life every day and every minute.

As usual, I stay at home and read in front of windows. A postman is jogging to deliver mail. Today, the weather is cold; the temperature is minus 9 to 13 degrees centigrade; plus the wind chill. He is always as busy as a beaver. I knew that he must love his career. Many people have their hour in history. It inspires from generations to generations. When he drove the car away, I felt in deep pondering.

First I should repent. I did not devote all my time to pursue my career. My worst habit is not thinking. My psychiatrist taught me that I should do housework 1 hour every day. I did not strictly follow his instructions. Our church let us read the book of Mormon every day, but I miss reading some days. Yet today, I did follow it and did it well. Last but not least, I obey God's words. Guard your heart at any moment.

Under God's love: Jesus said, 'Forgive, and you will be forgiven' (v.37b).

9

To God's Messenger

10

MM

Too many things happened. Margret is a widow now. She must pay attention to her behavior and avoid to talk to men. Sometimes she even feels it is a burden to go shopping! Today is April 1st; she is invited by her girlfriend for dinner. After dinner, they went out for a walk. In the elevator, Margret is seeing her face so bright under the light. She is surprised and delighted. In front of the gate, she is still obsessed in that moment and touches her face unconsciously while watching her reflection. Meanwhile, two condo workers come in-Tom and Jack. Tom is in the front. He suddenly saw her and pretended to drop the keys and picked up on the floor. His ass shows. Two girls shocked. Indeed, his ass is very white.

Doing this performance is not the first time for Tom. Many women in the condo are the elites in their fields. Yet Tom often can get a piece of ass for tips. He is thirty five years old and has a son. Money is always tight for this three persons' family. Women without sex and accompanies are plenty. Why not and just do it. As working convenient, he did not think too much for offering sex or going with women. He wanted to act like a real gentleman. He thought that this is a win-win situation. By the way his baby monster needs food and dignity. But today is an April Fools' Day. Margret is shy and felt she was wrong. No pain no gain. Tom also hammered himself and finished work earlier and headed home. ("I need more work done" is his secret code with his wife.) She knows. What can she do? She is a housewife. They love or may love each other, which is her belief.

Tom goes home. His wife is satisfied. They enjoy the supper on April 1st. This time is different, because he wants a change in his whole life, not because of Margret, but for many, many women.

11

Choices

Today is Sunday. Ashely and Michael drove to church. One thing is unusual-Ashely wears tight clothes and she is pregnant! Everybody says congratulations to them especially to Michael. Michael smiles in response to them, but in his heart, he is very curious. Who is the father of the baby?

The church's first section is the Sacrifice Meeting. Michael did not have any interest in listening. He has been a Sunday school teacher for months. He recalled several times Ashely told him that she was ill and then disappeared. They were married for many years and had no child. Both of them went to hospitals to check and they were ok. He sat there and dreamed how she demanded to hook up with him. Yet he was sure he did not ejaculate without a condom or even did not do it. He wished that he could have a child later. What's a big surprise! He thought about the future; he even thought about divorce. Yet facing the whole church, he admitted this mistake. He feared. To be honest, if his wife did not wear tight clothes today, he would not know about her pregnancy. Ashely sat beside Michael calmly. She enjoyed the people's blessing. For her, this is the first time she will become a mom; she is very happy. But she did not know who the father is either.

Ashely is a good girl. She was a Sunday school teacher too. She also grew up in the church just like Michael. They even married and sealed in our temple. She is eager to be a mother, however, Michael does not want to be a father so soon. She heard that Michael got the mumps when he was young. So she was very worried about it. Although the doctor said it is ok. She doubted it. Finally, she finds a family. They have two sons so far. They are all blondes. They are good people, but not rich. They understood Ashely, who wants to be a mom. Ashely gave them a sum of money and made love with the father. In the meantime, she did the same thing with Michael. In her own heart she always wishes that she is pregnant with her own husband.

Michael is not a fool! He soon found some buddies in church. He let them find who tangled with Ashely? Now he knew that family. He went there directly. They are much kinder than what he thought. Their children are lovely; but Michael could not trust them. He was very upset and went home. "Ashely you should go to the hospital for an abortion!" "NO" Ashely said. "We made love for many years! Why can I not get pregnant? If you are its father, I have no reason for an abortion. Michael is furious. He said that: "You want a baby; it is ok." In our church the Smith family have three sons and he is a doctor. Why you did not hook up with him? You feel shy, right? For God sake, I talk to them and let you be a real mother." Ashely did not dream that her husband could say that to insult her. She cried.

Michael is not joking! He immediately called the Smith family and drove there. He told what had happened and he pleaded! For God sake. This didn't surprise the Smith family. Many couples love Smith's sons and want to do so. He is not the first and won't be the last either. Smith said to Michael: "We are all men; you just fuck her like a bitch. Then you will have a beautiful baby. I promised." Smith told others the same thing. Now Michael knew how silly he had been. He grew up in the church. In his mind, he keeps love, service, toleration, respect, protection… for his wife. No one said that like Doctor Smith.

Michael goes home. He said to his wife "Please let us do it again."

12

West Country Style Party

Saturday, sometimes the church provides parties. This Saturday, we have the West Country Style Party. It is pot luck. Church members bring lots of food. The James family even gives everybody a cowboy hat! It really cheers us up.

Sister James is busy serving people. Brother James is a professional actor who is acting as a hunter now-Funny guy! He looks young and sexy. His fashion shoes have two stars on the top of each other. He shows them by upping the toes. More funny things happen; he wears a fake mustache. But when he eats something, he magically makes the mustache disappear! He does it several times. His wife sits beside him acting like nothing has happened.

The DJ plays music. Many people begin dancing, even kids. Our bishop reluctantly dances one line dance with us. He is too shy for this. He sits beside a teenager girl, and talks to her. Her sister is dancing now and very joyful.

Brother James holds the camera shooting the photos on the wall and doors. The photos are with "WANTED: REWARD". His hand even puts on the holster of a gun. His black hat, jacket and masculine fitting pants make him a perfect professional shooter. He even wears one piece of black glass-that is his true skill. At least, I cannot do it. Once he takes out his gun and pretends to shoot people. With music continuing, people take photos. Many people want to take photos with Brother James. He likes it too. I do not do it. I always avoid it. Many people also takes photos of the bishop and Brother Moore. They are all our major leaders. I saw that the church people are so delighted with the church and the leaders. I feel that I really follow the true church.

Finally, we have prizes for primary, young adults, adults and a grand prize. Brother James wins the grand prize. His prize is all kinds of fake mustaches. He is very surprised. I think that Sister James must leak some information to the organisers.

After the prize, we put back the tables and chairs. Some take left-overs home. We are still enjoying our party and wish tomorrow that we can see each other again. God's love is our church's philosophy. Volunteering is our daily work.

Wish our church was always like today. God bless us all.

13

ECHO

Today is the Toronto Canadian National Exhibition's opening day. Police come and deploy in the early morning. Some drive the police cars here; some ride bikes or walk; some even stay in the C.N.E. for the whole night. No matter where you go you can see them. Recently, Toronto often experiences a high crime rate so many people felt nervous. This year the C.N.E.'s employees are on strike, which makes the situation more complicated. The employees persuade people to not cross their picket line to go to C.N.E.

At 10:00 am, the Ontario Premier and the Toronto Mayor come. As one of the audience, I enjoyed Toronto police horse show and band performance. Sometimes you will feel funny; you see the police even more than civilians. A few leaders and organizers talked in the Opening ceremony; of course the Premier and the mayor also make speeches. Just one curtain behind the stage, strikers made all kinds of noise. Some are drumming; some are blowing; some are screaming; some are controlling the big balloons so that we can see the written slogans from the stage side. They are so loud that we even cannot hear the Premier and Mayor's speeches so well. That is Canada is so free and democratic for most of us.

C.N.E. has many fun games. Dogs shows; animals shows; opening play grounds; trading hall; Chinese lights shows; the food building; ice skating; and gambling hall. People scattered and enjoyed. At least I did. Police and securities patrol everywhere. We can feel safe and appreciate their protection. When I finished the play, I took the street car to go home.

Since today is the opening day for C.N.E., most of the police stations are working together to protect and prevent any possibilities. 52 Division is also one of them. One group of three policemen rode bicycles to patrol on the street. They have eagles' eyes and notice anyone's response to them. The policeman in the middle sees me on the street car and talks to the third policeman, who faces me and uses his right hand to clean the wax out of his ear and rub his nose. I see them. Many years ago, one police did rub his nose when facing me. I guess that they remind me to be safe. While on the street car the three policemen disappeared over the horizon. I will remember this occasion warmly and recall this in my heart land for ever.

14

Bananas

When I was young, I liked to eat bananas very much. At that time, I lived in China and we do not produce many bananas because the weather is too cold. So every time my relatives got together, they brought some bananas so that I would eat a lot. One of my uncles always blamed me for this, since at that time in China bananas are a kind of very expensive fruit.

In 2002 I immigrated to Canada to make a living. The first day I went shopping. I bought a lot of bananas for the reason that it is the cheapest fruit and the quality is the best-big and delicious. I still remembered that it cost 19 cents per pound. I carried them home and ate them for two days. At this point, I felt Canada is really heaven.

Time passed fast. Now I stay in Canada seventeen years. I have my own house and stable income. I often go shopping in supermarkets. I love fruit and always buy 3-5 different kinds of fruits at once. I seldom buy bananas anymore and do not get excited like I used to. I did not feel anything was wrong. One day I passed my neighbour's house. Through the kitchen's window, I saw a bunch of bananas on their counter and there was no other fruits. I was surprised and smiled as I went away. That day I went to supermarket to buy five different fruits, which including avocados that I seldom eat. I went home to eat my fruit. But the avocados were too raw. I did not consume. After a few days, they were rotten. I had to throw them away. I blamed myself that I should not buy so much fruit at one time and I should not laugh at my friendly neighbour either.

Last Sunday, I went to church. I go to church every Sunday. I walked in the church's corridor. I saw the bishop coming out from his office. He ate a banana. I was a little bit surprised! In my mind the bishop and some church high priesthood members are all rich people or fancy ones. Most of them were born in Canada. My bishop was born in London England. They also eat what we eat. I recalled our church's tithing. I believe that the bishop family pays tithing on time. They have money but do not laugh at the needy and like to help people. I feel I should be like them and never giggle at my neighbour anymore.

In western culture, they call Asian people who teach by white culture but yellow skin are banana men. I guess that my neighbour may want to teach their children this so they just let them eat bananas.

15

Encounter

In 2014-2015 year I finished a book. During this period, I experienced a lot. I was sick and stay in the hospital twice. I went to jail once since my psychiatrists sued me. During my jail time, I conflicted with the police. When I went home I wrote these unfair issues in my book. December 17th, 2015 it is my last time for bail. In order to show my anger or injustice, I chose December 16th, 2015 to publish my first book.

In the morning of December 17th, 2015, my husband and I went together to Toronto Old City Hall for bail. We took subway to Yonge and Bloor intersection to change subway. We took the electric escalator up. In the meantime, I saw TTC CEO Andy Byford walking down the stairs. I watched him for a while, he lowered his head and then disappeared in the crowd. I did not think too much. I felt that he may often show up in the public. After all I see him on TV or in the newspaper almost every day. We took the subway to Old City Hall. The judge announced that I was free. My husband and I felt very happy and went home. I recalled today's encounter many times. In my book, I did mention that I did not always pay for the TTC tickets for two years. I even began to be afraid of my behavior. Although the judge finally freed me, I just felt I did not deserved it. My actions were enough to go to jail…

Now it is 2019, Andy Byford went to New York City to be the President of the New York City Transit Authority. I may never see him face to face anymore. Many times I regretted that I should have greeted him when we met. Yet I was not sure whether he would mind or not. After all nobody in the crowd said anything to him. Sometimes I wish that I were his employee so I can be reverent and respectful and show my heart. On the other side, if I was his employee, when I went to bail, I meet him; it is not a good sign. He may fire me on the spot. Anyway, I am just an amateur writer. He is so successful and a big shot! He is just ten years older than me. Yet I feel he is forever my idol. Our encounter forever warned me to be good. Thank you Andy; thank you my friends who teach me how to be a better person.

16

Lady-like

This Monday, Margret's good friend and neighbour drove to Valley-tree store to return the counter's wheels. They stopped the car near the store. Coincidently, three policemen came out from a bar crossed the street. A fourth one went toward them. One of them is a strong, tall and handsome. He is popular, no matter whether he is wearing the uniform or not. Female or even transsexuals often offer sex to him. His nickname is called "but wiser". He feels cool and arrogant and did dress up.

Two girls dressed like boys. One with a baseball cap, one wears jeans. Margret lost weight recently, and she did not have money to buy some new clothes. She just can wear the saggy pants. On the top, both of them have long jackets. Nothing sounds wrong. Margret's one side collar of inside cloth shows. She never notices it. She likes police; she watches the three guys. In the meanwhile the tall one faced her to pull up his pants. Margret could feel his ignorant scorn.

To be honest, he always patrolled the Grill and Bar. There, who knows what kind of people he connected with each day? But today, he is useful. A simple case, a fashion girl in the bar and two sides of a few men fight for her. The owner called the police. But wiser was eager to go, he wanted to see what kind of alien can make it happen in a Toronto bar. He and another two policemen drove the police car there, he seldom hides himself. On the contrary, he always shows his positive side-his strength and body size. Both men and women all glance at him. Maybe because of this, he was promoted from foot patrol to car patrol. He could not forget today's girl in the bar, so beautiful. When they took the notes and said bye to the "lady"; he almost became a party animal! At this moment, he really tried to forget who he was and bring his trophy home.

He is single, yet his parents had taught him positively and strictly. He could not forget it spontaneously. Her wonderful body shape is just like a swan. She wears black instead of red to make him feel more mysterious. He felt thirsty, and really wants a bottle of "but wiser". His favorite brand is also his nick name. His colleague pats his back and they finally go out.

Toronto is so true. He just saw the woman he likes the most and wants her. Two tomboys show up. He puts on his sunglass and does the classic farewell-pull up the pants. Good work. He reluctantly parts from one and fires the opposite two. Margret felt sad; she knew that bars or concerts are not her strength. Also she builds her body shape. She still should not hang around there. Her girlfriend hates police for years because she always gets tickets. They drove the car home just like nothing happened.

17

Thank You

Another long night comes. I cannot read the books or study hard. The only thing I want to do is take the TTC to tour Toronto. Recently I have a boyfriend and dating costs a lot of money. Every time he leaves me; I feel very lonesome. I cannot handle it. At the beginning, I went outside walking. Now I prefer to take the TTC to enjoy Toronto's fantasy night life.

I watch the avenues with night lights. They are beautiful. Toronto is magnificent. I like Bay Street at night, which is all lights and skyscrapers. I like people on the streets too. Sometimes they are outside the bars or pubs waiting. Most of them are the younger generation. They seems very joyful. On the one hand I admire their life style; on the other hand, I really wish that they could study harder instead of wasting their time. I am old fashion. Now I even cannot persuade myself to work hard to improve my intellectual level. I can still recall that when I was young, if I did not study hard, my parents would beat me up. I wish that now somebody will discipline me to work harder too.

When I take the buses or street cars, I find that many individuals take the TTC without paying fares. I could not stop the temptation either. I learnt from them and dare go on the TTC for free. I look outside through the window. If I am tired, I sleep in the vehicle. I love this kind of life, which makes me happy. I get inspired and my curiosity gets satisfied too. Before then, I did not know that at night Toronto is so bustling. So many cars and people come out for their night life. I never think that now I am one of them and do not want to stay at home at night at all.

Today, I cannot forget. It is 12: 30 AM now. I went outside to begin my night life. I just pass the bus stop beside my house; one TTC bus stopped in front of me. I did not get on and continued to walk. I turned my head toward the bus driver; I saw that he wrote down something in his notebook. I was scared and deeply touched. I recalled what I did recently, I did not pay and abused the TTC. I am bad. Just at the beginning of this year, I had already made up my mind that I should pay my bus fare every time. Now I break my vow. The following night, I did not feel happy. I blamed myself a lot. The driver who wrote down the notes seems to be slapping me in the face. Suddenly, I woke up and repent what I did. I am wrong. Thank you TTC. Thank you the driver. Please supervise me at any time.

18

Take Notes

In my life, I still remember my first day in the University of Jilin China. I was very happy and proud to be a student of Jilin University. My first class was Shakespeare's Sonnets. I was not good at it and my teacher spoke endlessly. I was a little bit frustrated, since I could not understand very much. I hopelessly watched the teacher and sat there doing nothing. Suddenly, the teacher walked towards me and slapped my face hard. "Take notes," he shouted angrily. I felt my face become very hot and painful. All the classmates looked at me. I felt ashamed. I grabbed a pen and wrote down what the teacher was saying. My face was swelling. I covered my face with my left hand. I was humiliated. Yet that was my first class in University of Jilin.

From that day on, every time I listened to his class, I took notes. Sometimes I understood well, but I still took notes. Once when I did so, the teacher stood beside me and said that, "You already understand this part; why do you still take notes? You just write down what you do not understand." My teacher's care moved me. I lifted my head and watched him. I recalled my first day's behaviour; I did make a mistake. Meantime, I really wished that my professor would have told me my mistake after class. He might have gently given me a pen as a gift and told me take notes. His slap left a mark on my life, and I also hoped that I would do something in a different way. .

Time flies. I graduated from University of Jilin. I became a teacher. I teach at Jilin Adult High School. My subject is English literature. Here I noticed a girl whose name is Lisa. …She greeted me every day for a whole semester. In the new semester, she chose my class and sat down in the front row. She watched me and appreciated me, but I could tell that she did not remember a single word that I taught. Her innocent face looked toward me and saw me like a lover. I suddenly recalled my teacher in Jilin University. Should I do the same thing- slap in her face hard and let her learn a lesson? Yet since my teacher slapped my face, I already promised myself that if I were a teacher, I would not slap my students. I do not want to break my rule, especially since I am a man; she is a girl. Time passed. She still looked at me and did nothing. Now I can tell why my professor hit me. I walk toward Lisa and slap her face. She was very surprised. She lowered her head. "Take notes," I told her. She found a pen and took notes. I saw her red face. She also saw that I looked at her so she used her left hand to cover her left side of her face that I slapped. I spoke slowly, so that she could take notes. After class I walked up to her and said that "I am sorry." She shows me her notes. I corrected some mistakes. I told her seriously, "Study hard or get another slap, because you are very special to me."

19

Bear Skin

When I was young, I had a dream that I could hold a bear; a real bear, but I couldn't achieve the dream at the Toronto Zoo. My dream bear is a big kind and friendly grizzly bear. It is a male one because male bears are much bigger than female bears. Last Tuesday, our teacher Liz took us to AGO for a tour. I suddenly found my child's dream becoming true. I saw a bear skin on the tour. I touched the bear skin that made me feel comfortable and excited. In the bear skin's head there are two holes for bear's eyes. The bear's claws are even there. The bear's fur is black in colour and very thick. This bear is a middle size black bear, not a grizzly bear. I feel that the fur is a little bit rough to touch. I wish that I could lay on the whole skin, but I am not that lucky. They stop me from doing so. They believe that bears are their worship animal, so that people should not do blasphemy to bears. We should keep bears 'skin and cherish aboriginal culture and heritage. The black bear skin is in their culture. We need to respect and find some interesting points to remember them.

I did the research. I think that most people like the Disney film *Brother Bear*. **Brother Bear** *was a 2003 American animated* comedy-drama *film produced by* Walt Disney Feature Animation *and released by* Walt Disney Pictures. *It is the 44th* Disney animated feature film. *https://en.wikipedia.org/wiki/Brother_Bear.* **The** *primary* **meaning** *of* **the bear spirit animal** *is strength and confidence. Standing against adversity; taking action and leadership.* **The spirit** *of* **the bear** *indicates it's time for healing or using healing abilities to help yourself or others. May 23, 2016 https://www.google.com/search aboriginal+bear+meaning.*

Indigenous sometimes kill bears even polar bears to eat their meat and wear their skins to keep warm in winter. In the meantime, they also believe that bear is a kind of spiritual animal and also on their totem poles. Bear is the symbol of strength and leadership. They worship bears too. They also think that bears have healing power. Bears' bones can cure some diseases so they use them to make medications.

The polar bear is considered as the "Wise Teacher" as it shows how to survive in harsh conditions. https://www.magicalomaha.com/blog/Bear-Spirit-Animal

Now global warming is causing polar bears to dramatically losing their territory and their population are very low. We need to help them. Some aboriginals live in the polar bears territory, so they can become the first people to help polar bears.

For black bears, they experience Ecocide. Their natural habitat is disappearing fast. They become isolated and population is much lower than before. Protecting them is everybody's job. They are not just aboriginal's friend and spiritual leader. They are our treasure too. I believe that we should protect environment. The global warming is mostly because people do not care that *a gradual increase in the overall temperature of the earth's atmosphere is generally attributed to the greenhouse effect caused by increased levels of carbon dioxide, chlorofluorocarbons, and other pollutants.* https://www.nrdc.org/stories/global-warming-101. We should avoid globe warming from our own behaviour first. Both human beings and animals can benefit much from it.

Reference

https://en.wikipedia.org/wiki/Brother_Bear
https://www.google.com/search? aboriginal+bear+meaning
https://www.magicalomaha.com/blog/Bear-Spirit-Animal
https://www.nrdc.org/stories/global-warming-101

20

My Puppy Buddy

Buddy was born on the 25th, October 2019. I adopted him from his breeder on December 23rd, 2019. He is a German Sheppard puppy. When he was 8 weeks old, he was already 20 pounds. He is very handsome with black dominant color and brown legs and neck. He has very big paws. Most of people see him and say that. I gave his name "Buddy", because my cat name is Prince, and he is seven years and one month older than Buddy. I wish that he and my cat Prince could be good friends. When I just got Buddy, I told Buddy that from now on, Prince is the crown prince at my home; you are the body guard. Buddy is not happy about it. The first time he was at my home, he barked a lot at my cat. In the beginning, Prince tried to fight with him. Finally, Prince fled. He stayed in the basement for almost 2 months. I felt guilty for my cat. I love my Prince more. First day I walked Buddy, he was very upset. At that time, he could not climb and walk down the stairs. I forced him to go outside. The first day I walked him, I felt very surprised! Before then, I believed that every dog can walk outside and pee and poo outside too. Buddy did not like outdoor activities at all. He did not walk even one step. He sit and tried to go home. I felt that I was a fool and could not deal with a puppy. I held Buddy inside the home and he peed and pooed on my carpet.

Buddy always bites me with his sharp baby teeth which makes me bleed. His paw nails are sharp too. Sometimes, I felt very frustrated, since Buddy seldom listens to my orders. Buddy likes chewing wires. My two computer wires, two Sony head phone wires and four cellphone charger wires were cut off. I went to Best Buy to replace my computer wire. It cost over 56 dollars. I had no choice and bought a big cage for him.

Buddy likes fruit very much. His favorite fruit is water melon, just like me. He also likes plum, apple, apricot, dragon fruit, mango and cantaloupe. He also likes Chinese pancakes, which I often buy in Chinese restaurants. Buddy has many kinds of food. He has puppy food and adult dog food. The vet said that he grew too fast, so he needs to be eating some adult dog food to control his body size. Buddy also has treats and chewing milk bones, because his baby teeth need to become stronger and stronger.

Buddy likes to make friends. He always follows the strangers and plays with them. He is nice to them; by far, he has not bitten them. He does not like dogs very much and barks at them. I also make many friends because of Buddy. Some have their dogs; some are passersby. I never feel that I am so popular. That is the bonus Buddy bringing to me.

I chose Buddy mostly because he is a pure breed of German Sheppard Dog. Every time I watch TV and movies about police dogs; most of them are German Sheppard Dog. They are strong, smart and loyal to the masters. I hope that when Buddy grows up, he could protect me and be loyal to me. Buddy always gives me a wet kiss, and sometimes steals a kiss from me. Now I am really afraid of his biting.

Saturday February 8th, 2020, Buddy will go to his first training class, I wish that we could get straight A's.

21

Buddy's Training Class

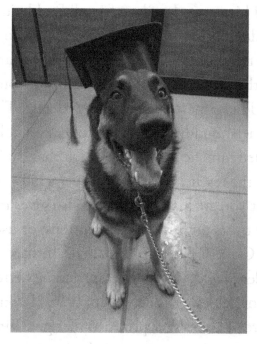

When I first got Buddy, my bishop told me that Buddy and I should go to puppy school to study. The bishop recommended Pet Smart to us for studying. Today, both of us attended the class.

I went there 1 hour earlier. The pet store is very busy. Many customers and workers smile at me and pat or feed my German Sheppard Buddy. He is very excited too. He is very friendly and shows his hospitality to them. I also feel very happy just like a successful mommy. They all said that Buddy is beautiful or handsome. Buddy plays with them like a toddler.

Soon the class began. The teacher is a lady. She is very cheerful and speaks loud, since some puppies are barking a lot, especially Buddy. The teacher said that if the dog barks too much, you can spray it with cold water, so it will stop barking. Buddy is very noisy. The teacher sprayed him twice, and he stopped barking. I laugh at Buddy.

Class 2: February 15, 2020, Buddy and I went to second class. We still came one and a half hour earlier. He played with a lot of dogs and humans. One is my neighbour. He recognised me but I do not know him. He said his home address and his name. I make a friend! Buddy jumps and jumps at the teacher. She sprays Buddy once. Buddy hurt his feelings, so he hid under the chair. The teacher uses the treats or calls him, but he is still shy and withdraws. I am a little bit sad for him. In the class, the teacher cheers up the puppies and teaches them "sit and leave it." Buddy is smart, so he learnt very fast. The teacher teaches puppies to run to their owners. Buddy directly ran to me, yet at last, he played with strangers. The teacher called him; he ignored her. I felt that Buddy is not loyal to me very much. At last, I ask the teacher why Buddy always bites me very hard. She said that, Buddy thinks that you are his siblings. She also gives me some tips to overcome it. For example: use treats to distract his attentions, or use water spray. Overall, I felt happy today.

Class 3: February 22, 2020, in this class the teacher teaches dogs to obey the order "lay down". He learnt fast. The teacher also teaches puppies to find their owners. Buddy is an expert at it. He only use 12 seconds finding me in the big store. The teacher prizes him. I give him treats too, yet Bubby ripped two bags of doggies' treats open. I show my wounds that Buddy bit me. Our classmates all have some wounds too. The teacher said to me that I can use water spray to control his bad behaviour.

Class 4: February 29, 2020, today, the teacher helps Buddy get into a harness, so I will not be afraid of hurting him, when I walk him. Buddy and I always go to school early. In the class, the teacher teaches puppies to bow. Every puppy does well. Then the teacher teaches them jump through the hoopla ring. One middle size puppy did it perfectly. The teacher cheers her up. Buddy is a little bit awkward; his back legs cannot jump that high. The teacher said that German Sheppard all have this problem. I am not happy about this. The last thing the teacher teaches is fetch. The small doggies use sticks. The owners throw the sticks and the puppies fetch. Their performances are pretty funny. Most often they do not go or do not know how to drop it. Buddy is a big boy, so he fetches tennis balls. He is stupid. He uses his mouth to hold a ball and goes everywhere. I call him to fetch another ball but he does not listen. Finally, under the teacher's assistant he brings 7 tennis balls back. Today, Buddy and I are all exhausted.

Class 5: March 7, 2020, today in the morning, I am still awake, so I go to Pet Smart at 9:40 am. The teacher even comes later than us. I shop in the store, and buy two salmon treats for dog and one fish treats for cat. It is expensive. They are my babies; they deserve these. Buddy is much stronger now, I almost cannot handle it. My finger nails are broken and bleeding a lot. He is still energetic; what can I say, a puppy. I outdoor watch the teacher teach the first class. I learn some skills. I feel happy. After the first class is our class. Buddy and I stay in the classroom. He pees there. The store clerk helps me to clean it. I walk Buddy in the store, he poos on the floor. I clean it. The teacher warns us, next time we cannot come too early. In today's class the teacher reviews the most important practice in the last 4 classes. For example: sit, down, bow, run to your owners, drop, leave it … she also teaches us how to touch the button. Buddy is not good at it. I do not feel happy for his performance. One thing I am satisfied is Buddy runs to me fast and loyal. The teacher praises him. Next class, it is our graduate ceremony. I will bring iPad to take pictures for Buddy.

Class 6: Today is June 20th, 2020. The class is postponed by COVID-19. I bring my new cellphone to take pictures of Buddy. Buddy is almost 8 months old now. He is over 80 pounds. I feel exhausted trying to control him. Our trainer is Tracy Simpson. I finally remember her name. Buddy sees his old classmates Marlow and Ode. One is 15 pounds and one is 8 pounds. Buddy plays with them and bullies them a lot. The other two did not show up. The trainer reviews all the skills. I am worried that Buddy needs to repeat the class. The teacher said that he is ok.

The Graduation Ceremony begins. First the teacher puts the biggest cap on Buddy's head. I let the teacher take photos of him and both of us. Today I also dress up for this exciting moment. Then the teacher puts the small caps for Marlow and Ode. They all take photos. Finally, the three of them have photos taken of them. The teacher issues Graduation Certificates for the three of them. I am satisfied with the Pet Smart's training classes. I like it because it is affordable, and has good trainers.

22

King Sheppard

In the training class, the teacher said that Buddy is probably a King Sheppard. This is my first time I heard King Sheppard. I went home and went on to the internet to check what does King Sheppard mean. <u>The **King Shepherd** is the true embodiment of "man's best friend," being a loyal, loving, and family-friendly crossbreed. This dog is a recently developed mix of the German **Shepherd** (GSD), the Shiloh **Shepherd**, and the Alaskan Malamute. (Jun 4, 2019) King Shepherds are very intelligent and energetic, and needs both challenging mental stimulation and plenty of exercise. The King Shepherd takes well to strenuous activity.</u> (https://en.wikipedia.org/wiki/King_Shepherd)

At the beginning, I even cried, because I really wanted a German Sheppard Dog. King Sheppard's life span is 10-11 years. German Sheppard's life span is thirteen years. I wish Buddy could accompany me as long as possible. In the morning, I called his breeder. The breeder said that Buddy's father is a King Sheppard; his mother is a German Sheppard Dog, so he is a crossbreed. He also said that Buddy's father is seven years old. I love Buddy no matter what. I stopped crying and fed him, then walked him outside.

My neighbours are very kind. They sometimes put some dog toys on my veranda. One dog toy is a rubber ball called "Chew King". Buddy loves it very much and chews it every day.

Now Buddy was proved with King's blood. Prince (my cat) is hiding in the basement every day. Just like my boyfriend said that Buddy one day will be a king in your home, because he is stronger than you and your cat Prince. I wish that Prince will get along with Buddy soon. I love both of them.

Reference:

www.k9web.com › breeds › king-shepherd
https://en.wikipedia.org/wiki/King_Shepherd

23

Caring for Buses and Street Cars

I take the Toronto Transit Commission to school every day. Some people especially less than thirty years old often put their shoes on the buses or street cars' seats. I like Toronto's transit. It makes it very convenient to go to work and come home. Even on weekends or holidays, we still enjoy TTC's services. Children do not need to pay and buses and street cars go everywhere. Every year the city of Toronto, Province of Ontario and federal government, spend almost eleven billion dollars for the TTC and public transit. We not only benefit it, but also protect it. Public transit is the city's symbol of civilization. When a stranger comes to Toronto, he or she may first use public transit. If he or she sees the dirty chairs, he or she will think our city is messy, backward and uncivilized. As a person, who loves our city, I wish everybody could protect our TTC and should not put their shoes on seats.

Caring for Buses and Street Cars

24

Bishop Philip Barker and I

Our bishop Philip Barker was born in London England. When he was young, his parents immigrated to Canada. Here he married and has four children. His elder daughter also has kids. He is the second English gentleman who I talk to. (The first one is my very good friend) Bishop Barker is very tall and his wife is tall too. Their children are all taller than me. He wears size M shirt. I give him one shirt every year. I like him because he is the first bishop to visit me when I was in the hospital. I have mental illness. I am a widow and no relatives live in Canada. Every time I am in hospital, I feel that I am dying. My father is in China and very sick. I felt hopeless. In 2017-2018, I stayed in hospital, the public guardian and trustee controlled my money and house. They even wanted to option my house. July 23rd, 2017 is my birthday. Bishop Barker visited me on my birthday. His coming deeply moved me. Besides my father, Bishop Barker still remembered my birthday and visited me in the mental illness hospital. He talked to me and comforted me. At last, I kneeled down; he kneeled down too and prayed.

Bishop Barker treats my family very good. When my husband was sick and stayed in hospital, he visited him more than once. I remember that first time the doctor informed me that my husband was dying. I told my church friend and within 1 hour, Bishop Barker went to hospital to visit my husband. His visit made me feel that I am not alone and Jesus Christ did send the right people to us. At that time, he did a silent prayer for my husband. One thing is a pity; my husband was in a coma and could not see the bishop. Hopefully, Bishop Barker's prayer would be heard by him. The second time, my husband was still in coma,

Bishop Barker and my husband's accountant visited him. The three of us talked about some important things including my husband's funeral. He praised me for taking care of my husband. When my husband passed away, Bishop Barker held a funeral in church. He even drives to the graveyard. My late husband's parents are also buried there. He did a prayer to them. Every time I recall this, I feel so warm and thanks to Bishop Barker.

Bishop Barker is very enthusiastic. He often says hi to us, likes to communicate to us, and holds parties in his home. He is a business man, but he would like to sacrifice his time and money to lead the church in a better way. I am comfortable under his protection. Sometimes, I make mistakes. He follows the church's rule to educate or constraint me. Once he even warned me that if I did not correct my faults, he would get rid of me from the church. I was very scared. I know that he is not only kind, but also strict. I love him just like loving my father.

Hi Bin,

This is a very kind letter. It was wonderful of you to share your thoughts with me. As Bishop, it was very challenging at times with all the responsibilities I had for so many people. So hearing this from you helps me to feel that my service has made a difference. Thanks so much for sharing this with me. I will keep it as part of my family history so that my children and grandchildren will know more about Bishop Barker when I am no longer here. Your husband was a wonderful person and the plan of salvation is very comforting to me. We will see him again one day. We are all God's children and we have a wonderful opportunity in the eternities if we choose to follow the Saviour Jesus Christ here on earth.

Have a great day!

Quotation from Bishop Philip Barker

25

My Boyfriend Danny

In February 9th, 2019, I met Danny Jamie Doyle in the Bayview Chapel of the Jesus Christ of Latter Day Saints. He was born in September 4th, 1963. He is a blondie and a big guy too. He has never married and has no children. He lives with and takes care of his mom. I like him. That day, he used his cellphone to watch the hockey games. I walked with him and asked him many questions. He is honest. I invited him to dance, but he said that he did not like to dance. I felt very happy, because I did not like to dance either. We talked about many things. His sense of humour and love of food made a deep impression on me. I left my phone number with him. He drove with his church's members here, one of who is my very good friend. He said that if I like, he would like to give me Danny's phone number. I remembered it. After this event, I waited for his phone call for a few days. Finally, I only can call my friend to ask for Danny's phone number. He gave it to me immediately. Then I called him. He is very naughty and said that he just wanted to call me and visit me on Valentine's Day. I felt released. On Valentine's Day, he went to my home. I gave him a T-shirt, which he likes. We went to a Chinese buffet to eat. There were a lot of customers. We spent 87 dollars. Danny drove me home. Then he said that he wished to see me soon. I agreed and decided that on Family Day we ate in China Town. That is our beginning of dating. From then on, we often see each other, sometimes 4 times a week.

We often see movies. He drives me to see drive-in movies. We sit in the car and watch movies. I like it very much. Danny often drives to some towns near Toronto. Lake Ontario is very beautiful. We go shopping together; we celebrate each other's birthdays. There are so many precious memories. Yet we cannot live together, since his mom is very sick and cannot live alone. Once Danny and I went to horse racing for gambling. The first time he went there to watch the horse racing with his mom and grandmother; he was just five years old. Once his grandmother gave him 2 dollars for gambling. Finally, he won 10 dollars! At that time, that was a big money. Since he dates me, he has never gone to Value Village to buy clothes. We go to factories' outlets to buy some good clothes.

Danny retired from Post Canada, when he was fifty five years old. He told me one episode. In his post office, there is a post man who is very stingy. They often gambled on hockey games. The loser should buy a cup of coffee for the winner. No one wants to bet a game with that stingy man. Danny once bet a game with him, because he thinks that it is just a cup of coffee, no big deal. The result is Danny wins. After one week, the stingy man still did not buy a coffee for Danny, which makes Danny very upset. He told other postmen and Danny laughed at him in public. The next day in the morning, he found that in his desk there is a cup of coffee there. Instead of buying, this coffee is from the across street funeral home which gives free morning coffee. Anyway, it is better than nothing. From then on, nobody ever bet games with that stingy man. After he retired, he enjoys his life every day. He is also a good handy man. If I have some house work I cannot do, I let him help me and I pay him. He is smart and hardworking. I am a little bit awkward.

The worse thing is that Danny always does not answer my phone calls. Once I have some urgent things, I called him 86 times one day, but he still did not reply to me. Finally, I gave up. Sometimes, I feel that I am deserted by him. I am so lonely and hopeless. That is why I adopted a puppy-Buddy. I am afraid of my future life. I lost my husband once; I was immersed in sorrow deeply. I wish that Danny can help and cheer up me. Yet, things are not as promising as I would like. I sincerely hope that Danny and I will be a couple in the near future.

26

Court

March 3rd, 2020 is my court day. I come to court three hours earlier. I sit on the bench and watch people. Some lawyers are very eye-catching. They use both oral and body languages to show their authority. One lawyer with a dirty backpack walks in front of me for a long time. He has a very thin cellphone and types some messages. Most people in the corridor use cellphones. When he looks at my dirty bag, I feel that we have something in common. One lawyer sits on the opposite side of the bench. He is showing off. He often uses terms talking to the police who helps him to keep a criminal locked up. He occasionally sees me. He likes playing with his tie. He loosens it and puts it back again. Once he watches me wearing a suit inside my jacket. He puts his jacket in his hands. I am shy, so I do not face him when taking off my jacket. I learn that in court I should wear my suit only. Lunch time comes. One lady crosses her legs and drinks juice and eats her sandwich. Her eyes often look at me. I just drink some Dr. Pepper (soft drink) and have no lunch which makes her laugh at me. I have no interest in seeing this kind of women. They have too much superiority. I also see a very huge man who does not eat lunch either. He and I are all clients I guess. I am out of date, I cannot use my cellphone to type and send messages. That is why I often carry a pencil box.

One short policewoman passes me which makes me feel much better. Some court staff are big too, so I do not feel alone anymore. One policewoman holds a "Roots" handbag; I think that she must has some special connection with the Toronto government. One lawyer always has his name in the paper. One lawyer always chats with others. I feel that some lawyers' time is not that precious. One court clerk wears black tie and walks straight. He must be very good in his work.

Life is full of opportunities from everywhere, at any time. People go from one side to the other side during a journey. I do not know most of lawyers in College Park, but I do remember one lawyer, who released me twice in mental illness court. I wish that I could see him today. A lady is standing in front of me and asks me if I need help. She comes from the Elizabeth Fry Toronto Agency. Her name is Diana. I talk to her and she helps and soothes me. She wears a suit that I like. I enjoy her help. She finds a key person in charge of my case. I explain to her that I did not touch my classmate' bottom or some place that he said to the police. I just did a wave in the air. I did not touch his body. I did not know why he is lying. Also, I do not want to have any sexual contact with a muslin guy. I also do not like a lower educated pauper. Please be respectful.

The school's monitor also has some problems. From different angles the camera will show different conclusions sometimes. So I highly recommend that we should not find just one monitor's picture to prove that I am guilty.

At the beginning, the lawyer watches the court DVD and says I am guilty. I need a lawyer. Yet I do not want to pay. I give my psychiatrist's letter to the court. I suggest that they transfer my case to mental illness court. They talk to the crown and the judge. They all agree. Finally, the judge cancels the charge and lets me talk to the social worker in March 26, 2020. I am free to go now. I wish my pen can win friends for me. I feel happy and walk to the elevator. A lawyer with a can of Dr. Pepper smiles to me. I feel that I win a friend.

27

Buddy Lost Friends

Today, I walk Buddy. He is very happy. We also see some friends who like to pat him. I do not know who threw some garbage. Buddy likes it very much. I am scared. It is just an empty package. If it has some poison in it, Buddy will die.

I walk him near my home. One senior pushes a buggy with two infants past us. I hold Buddy tightly. I am very worried about the senior and the babies near Buddy. I saw the senior's eyes are full of anger. I really do not know the reason. Buddy is friendly. He has many friends. Yet, for his safety, I decide that from now on, I walk him in my backyard. I do not want anybody to hurt him. Buddy cannot see his friends, both human and dogs, anymore. I hope that Buddy could grow up safely and healthy.

28

Police 11 Division

March 13th, 2020, I went to Walmart. I just wanted to jay-walk; one police car passed me and drove to the 7/11 store. For my curiosity, I followed them to the 7/11 store. I saw they drove the police car # 1111. I went to the Scotia Bank ATM to get cash. One police officer stood beside me. I asked him: "What are you doing here?" he smiled and said that he heated his lunch. When he held his lunch, I was astonished. That was a 284ml veggie soup. I saw the other box having 2 small pieces of frying fish in tempera. I asked him: "Is it your lunch?" he said that: "That is my buddy's". Their two persons' lunch is not enough for my own lunch. Even my dog eats more than that. Compared to them, I am really a pig! I immediately gave up eating in KFC today. As police, it is not easy. Many of them should diet, that is my least favourite thing. These two policemen, one is size "L"; the other is size "M". Police salaries are high. Many of them can earn over 100,000 per year. I also see lots of them eat in restaurants, especially Subway Restaurant, where they feel healthy. These two policemen bring their own lunch. They save money for their families and more. I also knew why I am fat. I would learn from them.

It was over 8:00 pm, I was very hungry. I did not know how long I could tolerate it? Eating less kills me.

29

Police 11 Division 2

Near Baby Point, there is a Note Bank coin shop. The owner is a handsome gentleman, who wins a lot of the opposite sex's hearts. Some are his regular customers, the others are his friends who often go to his shop to say hi to him. He knows who his favorites are.

If you have money, you will be a centre to some body. One neighbour in Annette Street planned to get a chunk. He is a notorious pimp with some homeless innocent girls. Some girls are really beautiful. He provides food to them to seduce the coin shop's owner. The two girls are in the final. One is the only one who can have money to buy a coin, the other is a pretty one but no money and just offers sex. The coin shop owner finds that so many ladies come to his shop; he is very confident. Yet they are all window shopping. He remembers one who often buys one coin. His shop's business hours and trends are all exposed to her. She is smart. The pretty one is simple, she seems that she only loves him. The owner has a couple of police friends necessary for business. The police already notice them but have no evidence. The shop twice lost coins even gold coins. The owner called the police, but they do not have some clues. He decided to find out by himself. He knows the pretty girl loves him but she is still shy. She is one of the leads. He makes love with her. He is already married and has one teenage son. His wife pretends nothing happened. Soon he knew who the culprit is. He can send the pretty girl to the police station, however he did not do so. He does not want to see her end up in jail. The owner calls his police friends to monitor the neighbour's cellphone messages and dialogue. Everything is fine. In March 18th, 2020 the police 11 Division police car # 1112 arrests him.

From the trial, the police even knew the culprit's plan B. One regular customer bought many coins and easy to steal from. They also want to sack her home, so the owner's customers might not want to come his shop to buy coins anymore.

Thank you police 11 Division.

30

Buddy in the Police Dog Academy

Buddy bit a neighbour! The police use a van driving him to the Police Dog Academy. I stay at home to pray that he will succeed.

There are over 50 dogs in the Toronto's Police Dog Academy. He is the only one called Buddy. His trainer likes his name, because the name "Buddy" is one of the Toronto original five police dogs' names. Buddy is good at running. He is in the top 3 for running. Buddy also likes jumping. Buddy's favorite task is biting. His teeth are just like a can opener. I believe that the Police Dog Academy will give Buddy a best job.

I miss Buddy very much, but I know I have made the right decision. One week has passed. At noon, one police car stopped in front of my door. Buddy comes back! I rush out and asked what happened. The police said that first we have enough police dogs; second, Buddy does not obey the orders, so his training is terminated. The Police car goes away. I hold Buddy tightly. I pat his hair to console him. I hold him and say "Welcome back Buddy!" Buddy is not disappointed, on the contrary, he is very happy and jumps here and there, just like before. My baby comes home. How sweet it is!

31

Public Guardian and Trustee

In 2017-2018, I stayed in a mental illness hospital 9 and ½ months. My investment and property belong to the Public Guardian and Trustee. Only four months, the Public Guardian and Trustee spent 22,000 dollars from my account. I got a free lawyer and fought back my investment and house.

Actually, I have a family accountant, who helps me pay bills and do investments. I really did not need a Public Guardian Trustee. They suck my money like crazy; some are even ridiculous! For example: the house belongs to government and I am a tenant. I need to pay money to them to rent my house. They hired cleaners to clean my basement, but I lost many things in the basement such as two water hoses and sprinkler, which were worth over 160 dollars. They even steal my late husband's brand new stamps for leather work. Some of my silver coins are missing. They charged me 89 times for only four months. For example, my cat was sent to a cat hotel for 2 months; it cost over 1, 000 dollars. I got my cat from the cat hotel in February 22th 2018, yet the public trustee worker charged my cat until February 23rd, 2018. They used my money to treat her friends. Annual management compensation at 0.60% equals $394.02, they charged me 4 times. I am totally being victimized within four months. In March 8th, 2018 I won the case to get my money and propriety back, but the public Guardian and Trustee continued to charge my money until April 30th, 2018, which cost me over 11,000 dollars.

Everybody knows that Public Guardian and Trustee is notorieties for their ridiculous charges, which makes their clients broke. I do not know why the Ontario government can tolerate this kind of agency to exist. It makes mentally ill people very scared and that they may lose everything. It is time to change!

32

Are You Lonesome Tonight

Are You Lonesome Tonight is Elvis Presley's song. I only know a few songs for many reasons, but I like this song very much. I have been sick for over two months and stay at home. Sometimes I even cannot walk my puppy outside. My puppy is over 40 pounds. Tonight, I could not stop coughing. I felt very uncomfortable and tried to vomit. I have chest pain and a headache. Last week, I went to the hospital emergency 3 times. They tested for COVID-19; the result was negative. They said that I should not go to the hospital again, because my illness is not an emergency. My boyfriend did not connect with me for almost 2 months. During this two months, I was sick 3 times. I struggled to live. He said that "We are friends but not boyfriend and girlfriend". Our church services stopped. I feel fatigue all the time and have no energy to wash dishes for many days. I do not have family members and relatives in Canada. The only two dependents are my puppy "Buddy" and my cat "Prince". They occasionally fight together.

I am forty four years old, yet I feel like I am over sixty years old in poor health. Night is quiet and long; especially as I am a widow. I am afraid of lying in bed, I always miss my late husband-slept in bed and held each other. I have some friends here. They knew that I am coughing so they did not want to visit me for safety reasons. My doctor said that I got seasonal allergies, which do not spread to others. Tuesday, my family doctor usually does not work. She is worried about me and called me to see her. She exams me carefully, and gives me the new prescription. She said that after two days to come to see her again. I appreciate her. Her action has truly moved me. I feel I am not so lonely.

My beloved husband passed away four years ago. I visit our graveyard at least once a year. He is part of me. He used his sense of humor to teach me a lot of morals. Once I stole 2 pens from our club. When I went home, he found them. He held the pens and said that, "These pens were stolen by Lisa from Progress Place." Every time, when he saw them, he said so; he wished that I could remember it forever. He was also my good mentor and best friend.

Easter holiday is coming. I wish that every person alive and dead are missed and dream of each other.

33

For Au Lang Syne

I have a very good friend who is a Turkish-Canadian. We did not contact each other for over one year, just because of a little bit of a misunderstanding.

I often treat her in Chinese restaurants. She is a Muslim. We avoid pork for sure. Once I treated her to a Chinese hot-pot buffet. We ate lamb and beef which was very delicious. Also it was expensive. Yet when I went home, she called me and said that the restaurant was not clean. I felt that she hurt my feelings. Then after a while, she said that she would not go to Chinatown to eat any more. She never treats me in any restaurant, but her daughter and she always go to very expensive restaurants to eat. Once they went to a five star hotel's top floor revolving restaurant to consume. They spent $ 280 dollars just for a dinner. I make friends with her for following reasons. She can speak mandarin well. She went to China to study for three years when she was young. She is good at cooking and very clean. I like her food, especially Turkish dishes. Secondly, she is a handicapped with a wheelchair. I had mental illness. We all need friends to socialize. She attended my wedding and gave me very good wedding gifts. Yet she never let me meet her daughter and did not even tell me her daughter's name! I am a woman too. I do not know why she is afraid of me? I am never pregnant and a widow. I believe in Christianity. I am not bad at all. During this one year we were separated, I think a lot. At the beginning, I blamed her more. I feel that she is stringy and selfish. I even think that Muslims are hard to deal with. I began to avoid any contact with Muslims. After a few months, I felt lonely, I started to recall our friendship. She taught me common sense and how to avoid danger especially for women and the handicapped. Sometimes,

I enjoyed her care; she is just like my aunt. My aunts did not teach me that much. We are friends over twelve years. She is good at knitting. She gave me many hats, scarfs and other things. She is a much better lady for domestic work than I. I never did knitting in my whole life. I am glad that I finally called her and renewed our relationship. I learnt to cherish love and friendship, although sometimes it is really hard. My morality is wider than treating others and strict with myself. Also I should understand the points of view of other different cultures.

Today, she went to my home and brought Chinese dim sum to me and one of our mutual friends. Just like before, I pay for the materials and she cooks the food. She is very happy and talked to my friend in English. She can speak 5 languages. I admire her. She brought some Turkish dry food for me. Some I never tasted before. Our mutual friend Mervyn likes this dim sum very much. He ate almost 20. Finally, I show my puppy Buddy to my Turkish friend. She is very scared and even did not pat Buddy. I put Buddy back in his cage. Then I saw her off to the bus stop. Friends should be for Au Lang Syne.

A few days passed. She and I tried to join together. My soy sauce was consumed. I wanted to buy it, but she was eager to buy it for me. I agreed and told her what kind of soy sauce I needed. When we got together, she showed me the soy sauce exactly that was the opposite of the kind I told her to buy. She asked me for $ 3.00 and I gave it to her. I remember in Chinatown I saw this soy sauce, nobody even asked for it. When the three of us ate the lame meat pie, I felt very disappointed. It is had almost no meat at all in it. She used carrot and beet instead of pumpkin. I could not chew the filling. One pie I ate, it even had a hard core of date. I remembered that I gave her a bag of dates. I almost broke my tooth. At the beginning, I only cursed my bad luck. I even trusted her again and gave her another 65 dollars for the next time together. She took it. My dog mistook a meat pie and soon had diarrhea. I knew there was something wrong with the lame meat pie. I threw out the last one. I called her. I told her the $65 was for her to enjoy. I promised her that if her daughter drew a painting and gave me the photo, I would put it in my new book, I will treat her mother for food. She is begging to cook more food for me. I refused. She called me again, yet I could not let her walk into my life again. She is a piece of garbage.

34

Foodie Emotions

I like to eat in restaurants, especially in Chinese restaurants. One of my favorite restaurants is Homemade Ramen at 263 Spadina Ave, Toronto. Since March, because of COVID-19, it is closed. I felt sad, because I cannot eat my favorite food Cold Steamed Noodles. I like this dish because it is very delicious and inexpensive (5.99 + tax, one bowl). Just beside this restaurant 261 Spadian Avenue, there is another restaurant whose name is Green Tea Canteen. I sometimes go there to eat. I am a member of this restaurant, the membership card costs 20 dollars.

Today, I am happy and have nothing to do. I decided to go to Green Tea Canteen to order food. We cannot eat in the restaurant yet. I take the TTC to Chinatown. I found that Homemade Ramen Restaurant is open. I come in and order my favorite food Cold Steamed Noodles. Then I go to Green Tea Canteen, I order Abalone with Marinated Pork 34.99 + tax, which is the membership price, if you are not member, the price is 36.99 + tax. I also order Dongpo Pork, which is 15.99 + tax. The non-membership price is 17.99 + tax. This two dishes cost me over 57 dollars.

I am very happy and rush home. When I eat at home, I feel disappointed. The Cold Steamed Noodles' quantity is not as big as before. The sauces are not delicious or are too spicy. The overall taste is no good. The Dongpo Pork is not as beautiful as it is in the plate. The taste is awful. It is greasy, too sweet and too fat. The Abalone with Marinated Pork is my least favorite. Six small abalones are smaller than quail eggs. Also the abalones are not fresh. They are all canned food. The taste is like nothing. I do not feel that it is fresh and tasty.

During the COVID-19, I spend most of my time at home. I always dream that I will enjoy my life just like before. As a foodie, my dream is to taste all kinds of delicious food. I even went to school to study culinary class. My teacher likes me and always teaches me more. He said that I am the best in the class. Finally, he gives me 81 score. I cannot forget him, as he is one of my favorite teachers forever.

As a foodie, I am very proud of living in Toronto. Here I can taste most countries' foods. Friends let us join in this foodie team.

35

What a Family

Siyuan He and her mother

My name is Siyuan He (思源　何), which is from yinshui siyuan (饮水思源).

It means when one drinks water, one must not forget where it comes from; remember those who fought to make the present possible for us;　gratitude for the source of benefits;　never forget where one's happiness comes from. https://baike.baidu.com/item/ I am a Chinese girl. I am twelve years old. As the youngest member in my family, I would like to introduce my family to you.

I live with my grandmother from my mother's side. She is seventy two years old and in good health. I like to eat fried rice made by her. My grandma's fried rice is delicious. She is the master cook in my family. My grandfather from my mother's side passed away just three days before I was born. My mother said that he was very gentle. He was retired, but he found a part-time job so as to earn more money for the whole family. He was killed in an accident. I hoped that my grandpa was still alive. I could see him every day. My grandparents from my father's side are farmers. I seldom see them. My mother is an English teacher. She is very strict, but very democratic. My dad has always blamed me for years, because he has a bad tempter.

Now let me tell you something about myself. I am a child who loves literature and art. I can paint, and I am very good at it. I can paint colour, lead, sketch, hand-paint, and Chinese paintings. Especially Chinese painting, I think everyone knows the painter Qi Baishi! He is very famous; he is the king of Chinese painting artists! He has been deceased for many years, but he has a descendant who taught me. This 80-year-old man is the third generation of Qi Baishi's disciples, then I am the fourth generation of disciples. I also sing well, and I can play Guzheng. Guzheng is a national musical instrument in China. It sounds very crisp and nice. It is just like gurgling water. I have a lot of certificates; I won the provincial awards in painting posters. I danced in the Spring Festival Gala! I have to thank my mother for nurturing me. I am very lively, like to talk, and have temper tantrums. I am always upset and unsure. I am weak and sick. I am kind and sympathetic to old men and beggars. I really want to give money to them. Seeing them makes me sad. My eyebrows are thick and my eyelashes are long. Others say that I look pretty, but I don't think so.

I am in a happy in Grade 6 Class 5. My current teacher is Mr. Deng, who is a Mandarin language teacher. He is our head teacher too. He is very strict with us, some classmates are afraid of him, but he is very fair, unlike my former teacher. He treats me very well. He always praises me. In class, he always asks me to answer questions. My English teacher is Teacher Song. She is very kind and has a good level of English. She also likes me very much, and my English is very good. She always calls me to speak in class. I always answer her questions. Then she smiles at me and everyone laughs. I like her class best. My math teacher is young and beautiful. Yet, her teaching skills are limited.

My family conditions are average, financially very tight, and cannot compare with the rich. We have no background and no rights. I'm used to an environment that lacks care. You see me very lively, but there is an indelible shadow in my heart. That's my story from the first grade to the fifth grade. The head teacher in grades one to five was a female Mandarin language teacher. She deliberately made it difficult for five years. She always slandered me deliberately and misunderstood me. In this way, the classmates also think that I am a bad girl. In the past five years, I have suffered a lot of wrongs. Why is this so? This is the case. My family opened a supermarket a few years ago. There is a lot of room upstairs that is not operating. A vice-principal of our school discovered this. He wants to use this to open an extracurricular study class. But my landlord who is not in the house has no cooperation to rent a house to him. He misunderstood our family. Then I retaliated with this class teacher and I became the victim of this matter. This is absolutely impossible in Western society.

The eaves on my roof are damaged, with a lot of less bricks and tiles. One drop of rain, two drops of rain, wet my clothes; three drops of rain, four drops of rain, washed away my joy, brought me endless sorrow; lightning, scared me away. This, I can't resist. This room is so big that I really can't get out. Without doors and windows, I have been wandering in this dark world. Finally one day, the roof shed a very strong light, and doors and windows appeared. I walked out of this dark world, facing the sunlight, and felt the warmth of nature. I am no longer afraid. However, that dark world is still floating in my head.

I love small animals very much, they all say that animals are good friends of people, and I think this is true. On New Year's Day last year, my mother bought me a small parrot from Qingyifang, with green feathers and blue tails, and black eyes. It was very beautiful. I named it "Jasmine". I played with it for a while every day. Sometimes I put my finger in the cage and it will stand on my hand and peck with its small mouth. It was so cute. In the morning after a month, it became fat, the hair was tied up, and its head was buried in the trough. I thought it was sleeping at first, and then I learned that it was sick, and it became fatter and fatter. At noon the parrot passed away. At that time, I was crying that I couldn't save it. In the evening, I buried it in the mound outside and set up a small tombstone. When I think about it, I go to see it. On the first day of Chinese festival of New Year, I was very sad throughout the New Year... One day on my way home from school, I heard someone tweeting about this on the dirt slope of Teddy. A few flies fell on her body, and an unpleasant smell came out. I take it to animal hospital. It was not cured until late at night. It left the world the next morning, and I was really sad. I hope everyone can care about animals and cherish life. Also, I wish one day I could have my own dog. (My mom is afraid of animals and does not permit me to have them.)

One month ago, I already wanted to go to the zoo. Yet until now, I still have not visited it. Today is Saturday. Thank God, it is weekend again. I wake up in the early morning to study. I do not have breakfast. I am also very busy in the afternoon. Sunday, I will be even busier. Monday I will come back to school until Friday. Then the circle repeats. So, I cannot go to the zoo for good. I often see other students going with their families here and there, I feel sorry for myself. This weekend I cannot go to the zoo for sure. It is not once or twice...

This is my family stories. I write it down and share these with all of you.

Siyuan He writes this story. Bin Sobchuk edits it.

Reference:

https://baike.baidu.com/item/

36

I Miss You

At night, I cannot sleep. I take the TTC for my long night journey. I take bus 40 to Dundas West Subway Station. I saw an acquaintance, who just wants to take the 504 street car. I pat him and said big guy! He remembers me and nods his head with a smile. He is a big guy. He is over 300 pounds. Near my home, I sometimes go to the Runnymede United Church. We meet each other there. I am a member there. Our church has a dinner on the last Saturday of every month. I have a dinner there and he goes there too. Once, on a cold winter day, he came with torn pants. His underwear even showed. He was very embarrassed. I saw it. I was very sorry for him. I am heavy too and 270 pounds. I know that people just like us find it hard to buy suitable clothes. Also the clothes are much more expensive than the regular ones. I was thinking I should give him 20 dollars for his new pants. Or next time I should give it to him. But he had already gone. After one month, I saw him again. He had new pants. I felt relieved and chatted with him. He is single and no kids. He is always happy; he is a security. After we broke the ice; we always talk to each other. Now with COVID-19, the dinner has been canceled. We had not seen each other for a long time. Today we meet again. Both of us feel happy.

I take 505 street car to Broadview Subway Station. When the street car passes Yonge Street, a man gets on the street car and sits opposite to me. I recognize him. He is a member of our Rehabilitation Club. He immediate knows me. He said that he is so sad. Since March, the members could not go to our club. The workers are in the Club House and listen to our phone calls. He misses our activities such as karaoke, movie night, Bingo, food preparation etc. He also said that he misses our members. We joke together and make friends. Actually, I met my late husband in our Club House. Our Club House is open 365 days in a whole year. Weekdays open at 8am to 8pm. Weekends and holidays open at 11 am to 8pm. He wears a beard. I find that a lot of men have beards since COVID-19. He drinks a 2 L Coca Cola. I drink a 710 ml Coca Cola. He is poor and uses a shoe box to beg for money. He writes that his family needs money and is hungry. Please help me. I give him 1 dollar.

Now I recall that one of my friends abuses our relationship. She buys and cooks a big rabbit. I pay the money for the rabbit. She does not want me to eat in her home. She said that we will eat on a lawn. She let me bring a bottle of Chinese spice. She said that she did not have extra money and time to buy it. She even does not want me to use her washroom. I annoyed with her. The Chinese spice is just 2 dollars and 50 cents. I do not mind anymore.

90% of my income is from stocks. Now the stocks are very low. Some companies stop paying the dividends. Also I adopt a German Sheppard puppy. So I feel that my money is tight. Sometimes it is hard to decide which one is more important. Friends or money?

37

To Ontario Government

My name is Bin Sobchuk. I am an adult high school student in Ontario; I am an immigrant to Canada and I was born in P. R. China. Neither English nor French are my first language. I find that in Toronto if you do not speak English well, it is hard to find a good job and keep it. That is why I chose to study English in school and why I choose to support teachers to maintain their jobs.

In an April 4th, 2019 article in the *Toronto Star*, the Ontario government has cut 3,475 teaching positions in four years. As an adult high school student, I do not agree with the government decision. We all know that knowledge is power. Teachers are spreaders of knowledge. Students learn knowledge and use it to enhance their positions and change our society. Teachers should not be short-changed. They are the foundation of our schools and basic productive forces of our society. They should not be cut; on the contrary, they should be increased in number gradually.

The directors of education and senior business officials in the province's school boards all plan to cut teachers. I doubt that they wanted to cut their own positions? If they believe that they are very important, they should ask society, who is more useful and directly impacts every family? The government officers want to bully teachers and use their salaries ($851 million) to do other things. It is really unfair and intolerant.

I call on you to support the Ontario teachers, the families who have kids in school, and the parents who want their children to study well. If teachers are cut, the classes will be bigger than before. The teachers will have less time to take care of the children. Children will fall in their achievement. The best way to stop the government is to show your opposition! Let everybody act to protect our teachers. I wish that Dr. Malloy would stop supporting cutting teachers.

38

My Veterinarian Saini

In April 2013, first day I lived with my husband; he brought me and my kitty Prince to the veterinarian near our home. That was my first time to meet our vet Saini. His English is very well. He is handsome too. I saw him like an Indian gentleman. I asked him where he is from. He said Punjab India. He is a skilled immigrant. He was a vet in India. Then I joked with him whether or not he remembered China and India had fought in 1960's. He said yes. I smiled and said that China won the battles. He smiled too and announced that India won the territory. Saini gave my kitty a needle for RABIES and some medicine for treating his worms. He charged a reasonable fee. Saini has been our pets' family doctor before I met my husband. He had a cat whose name is Harry.

Saini is very generous. He always charges less than the regular prices. Two or three dollars less almost every time. Sometimes he even reduces more than 30 dollars, at least he treats me like that. I am very appreciated of him. Once he cleaned my puppy's ear infection for free. He also cut my puppy's nails for free. He is not rich. He just hopes that the animals can go to the hospital when they need him. Not just like other vets, he does not have assistants or nurses. If it is emergency, he will call the schools to send a student to help him. He has not had the pets in his clinic. Once I asked him why you did not have pets. His answer was very humorous. He said that he has two pets, his son and his daughter. I saw his son and daughter a couple of times in the clinic. They are happy and proud of their father.

Saini is an expert in his field. He knows his clients very well. He diagnoses diseases fast and accurate. Now we have computers. We can check online before we go to the vet. Sometimes we can know the diseases, but sometimes the vets diagnose more professionally. Saini always tells me how he diagnoses the illnesses. He also knew the animals' psychology. He acts very fast. He never failed in my cases and saved me a lot of time and money.

Today, I saw a dead raccoon outside the gym. Crossing the street, the construction workers are building an apartment building. This is not the first time the construction workers have killed raccoons. Last month they killed a very big raccoon that was over 30 pounds. They threw it on the gym sidewalk. For over 1 week, nobody cleaned the raccoon's body. It stank and a lot of flies were on it. Finally the gym worker cleaned up the mess. Today, the dead raccoon is younger and smaller than the first one. It looked like it weighed 20 pounds. I saw that its fur very shining and it was fresh too. I recalled my late husband's nickname was raccoon. Our home even had a raccoon's fur hat. I wish that I could taste its meat and bones too. I felt that I should do something to keep it forever. I called my vet. I text message said that "I want you to peel a dead raccoon's fur." He replied that "Sorry, I cannot. As I am not allowed to do that. But" I did not think too much and replied "How much". He did not answer. I called him. He was very polite and refused to do the illegal deal. I felt sorry. I am a silly person who do not know our laws. Saini is a very good vet who really is not lured by money.

Recently, I saw he had white beard. He is bald too. I asked him what is wrong. He said calmly, "I become old." He is two years older than me. My hair is already white. I really hope that he will be our vet for a long time. We all like him.

39

Forever Police Force

Mark is a police constable in the Toronto Police 11 Division. He is young and has been on the police force only two years. His salary is not high. He broke up with his girlfriend recently. In the morning, he opened his eyes. Another sleepless night he had experienced. He rubbed his eyes and rushed to the police station. As police, they often work overtime; sometimes they even work 24 hours in one day. This also leads to having insomnia. He likes to go to police stations. There he has many brothers. He likes women police too, but brothers' love in his mind is more important. He and another police officer drive number 1103 police car on patrol. Mark is tired and almost happened on an incident. His co-worker stopped the car. They talk together. Mark is shy and tries to avoid telling that he separated with his girlfriend, which makes him depressed and hard to sleep. He cannot bear being alone. That is why he likes the cop shop. He loves his career. He knew that he can change people's lives and make the world peaceful. After a short chat, his co-worker drives the police car with him on patrol.

After work, Mark went home directly. He hopes that his girlfriend will come back into his life. Yet his reserve stops him from contacting her. Mark likes to help people especially crying women. He always shows sympathy to them. His girlfriend did not drop tears when they parted. He felt insulted. He called his police fellows. They go out for dinner. They drink beers. He suddenly socked in happiness. The police station is like a big family. They experience life and die together. Police are also the biggest gangs. One loses, others lose too; one wins, all win. They have some rotten apples. Get rid of them. The police force will be stronger and more glorious.

We need the police and give them time to show their better actions in the future.

40

Struggle

If you ask me who the most struggling people are during the COVID-19 period, I will tell you "Sex workers". In Toronto at Queen Street and Ossington Avenue, there is the largest mental illness hospital in the whole world. Some mental illness people who lose their working abilities, could not find a way to make a living, or do not want to work for other reasons, become Sex workers. Lily is one of them. Today, she took a shower in a shelter. She did not eat in the shelter, because her stomach is aching from the food that she ate last night in the shelter.

She went to a bus stop; she has no penny to buy make-up. She holds a bottle of water. She got it from shelter 3 days ago and refilled the water many times.

Lily sees some old customers on the streets, but they did not say hi to her today.

Lily is slim, partly because she also takes street drugs. Now she has not taken street drug for months, the reason why is that she has no money even a penny. Today she is lucky. One man stopped in front of her and they are bargaining. The man offers one buck for jiggy; she said two dollars. The man ignores her and wants to go. She begged him and said that you can do it as long as you want. Deal. This is Lily's life. Who would believe that it happens in Toronto now! Premier Doug Ford reduces disability pensions. Many with disabilities cannot find a place to live, so they live in shelters or on the streets. They need apartments to live, but who cares about them.

They are not alone. Let us go to Church Street. This is one of the homosexual and Sex workers centres in Toronto. Since March 2020, the bars and strip dance cinemas had been closed. They lost all their income. A few of them can get government COVID-19 financial aid. Most of them have no income. Lou is a victim. He is strong and very sexy. He is a black man from Africa. His daily job is to perform in men's strip clubs. He is popular and well known. His penis is over 10 inch. His nick name is "Black Hurricane". Yet in COVID-19 time, most people stay at home to avoid catching virus. His partner (a man) who lives with him lost his job too. Lou's many friends are black. In their eyes, Lou is powerful and generous. Lou does not have too much savings. He helps his poor friends and fellows. He and his partner finally decided to do drug trafficking. COVID-19 makes the streets empty; yet police cars often patrol the streets. Lou and his partner noticed. Their customers are limited but stable. They do believe that it is a good way to make money. They are new to this deal. Some old drug dealers try to destroy them. They call the police. Tonight, Lou and his partner met the police.

They used the car to try to escape, yet 3 police cars stopped them. Lou was pushed out to the car by his partner. His partner crashed the car into a police car. Lou escaped. He is afraid to go home and cried. He lost his partner and dignity. He becomes a true victim of COVID-19.

Who will help the weak part of the society? We need more help, let's unite and fight to win our dignity and rights!

41

Blessing

James graduated from the University of Toronto. His major was Criminology and Sociolegal Studies. He was awarded Honor Bachelor Degree. Then he went to the police academy and became a Toronto police officer. He works in Toronto Police 11 Division, where many Toronto Chief of Police came from.

Annie is a policewoman. She also works in the same division with James. They are the same age. But she joined police force before he did. She is 167 cm tall. She is not a blondie; invisible minority. She is pretty. Police force is 70% men. She did not lack men pursuing her. James is one of the men who are chasing her. He always acts like her older brother, works with her and protects her.

Today, at the St. Clair and Runnymede Walmart, Toronto police are investigating after the fatal daylight shooting in the Walmart parking lot. Half of 11 Division came there and blocked the parking lot. They interviewed witnesses, and encouraged people to provide leads about the shooter and the victim. Most of the parking lot were blocked by police. The police supervisor asked who wanted to patrol. James responded that he and Annie would like to. Annie was shy and did not say anything. James is very happy. He walks in front of Annie. Annie watches the parking lot carefully. She also recalled James had visited her home. One month ago, James asked Annie to go to her home to celebrate her father's birthday. Annie agreed. She did not want to hurt his feelings. James thought how to make her father like him. Finally, he decided to give her father $2,000 dollars of his overtime salary to please him. James hopes that her father will like him and agree to their marriage. Her father was astonished by the money. He saw the young man 175 cm high; he hesitated. He is 180 cm. James suddenly sneezed once, twice, and three times. *One sneeze means something good has been said, two means something bad has been said, three is a sign that someone is in love with you.* (https://www.ceenta. com/news-blog/6-myths-superstitions-and-more-about-sneezing) Annie smiled and said that "bless you". Annie's parents saw it and nodded.

They are dating and working together during the following month. James often works more to help Annie. His co-workers all make fun of him. "Hi, Jimmy, do you need to work overtime this week? Your father-in-law was bribed by you." James is proud to say that "I got Annie because I knew magic!"

Reference:

https://www.ceenta.com/news-blog/6-myths-superstitions-and-more-about-sneezing

42

Will

Will was a comedy actor and instructor who did improvisation for over fifteen years at the Second City. His talents were mainly from his parents' influence and genes. His father was a bishop of Jesus Christ of Latter Day Saints. His mother was a director who had done performances from the ages of fifteen years old to seventy three years old. He and his two brothers also had been bishops in the same church. His belief and religious knowledge were the strong sources of his improvisation. He graduated from University of Calgary etc. On the stage, he is very funny. His voice and body language can be changed quickly. His best characters are gentlemen and rogues. As a bishop, he is a good model, but with the same suit, he could change to a rogue with whistling, holding a stick, and walking style. Off stage, he is very quiet. His 5 kids are like him too.

Will corrected me sometimes. I am afraid of him. His mother Madam Will teaches by example to me many times. I must say thank you. I like to talk to people. Once I asked him why his wedding ring is a black rubber ring. He said that it is fireman's ring. His wedding ring sometimes is loose and sometimes is tight, with his weight's losses and gains. He is also allergic to gold and silver. Will is under great pressure in his life and career. Mrs. Will takes care of family all the time. His success partly belongs to her effects. I hope that I can find a good man to take care of me, so I will not experience too much difficulty. Although I am forty five years old, I am never pregnant. I heard that pregnant women maybe cannot fit their wedding rings either. As a widow, I should obey church's Doctrine and Covenants.

Will is a blondie. Some of his children are the same as him. Will's skin is quite white, just like a boiled egg white. Now he is a Deputy of Director in Art Gallery of Ontario. He likes his career. God bless him and his family.

43

Ontario Lakeshore

I like Lake Ontario. It is so big and just like a sea. I love its lakeshore, which makes me calm and I have a lot of fun.

Today, I called my friend to the lakeshore. Now it is October 14, 2020. The weather is a little bit chilly. My friend treated me very good. She cooked fried rice with eggs, beats, salmon fish and potatoes etc. She also bought a XL cup of coffee for me. My religion does not permit me to drink coffee, but she already bought it. I drank it. We face the lake to eat. I feel that I am in heaven! I have friend to accompany me and I do not think too much of trouble. I like the birds and animals. They make the lake vivid. She brought some bread to feed birds. They fight for it. I laugh at them. My favorite animal is a dog. When they pass me, I greeted all the dogs. Most of dog owners smile at me. Some let me pat and kiss their dogs. I also tell them that I have a dog, but he is in the training school. I cannot bring him here. The weather is not warm so just a few dogs swim in the lake. The owners only let them swim a short time. My friend likes the buildings in lakeshore. I do not travel too much. In the lake, there are many sailing boats. Some disappeared over the horizon.

Many years ago, in November, I committed suicide in Lake Ontario. I wear a jacket and swam to the break wall in the early morning. I saw the other side of the lake; I was scared. I stand on the break wall in the sunshine. A woman was rowing and passed by me. She even did not see me. I said hello to her. She ignored me and rowed away. I did not know what I should do. I walked on the break wall. I saw the cars on the streets and people walked on the lakeshore. Finally, I began to swim back. When I swam back to the shore. An ambulance and a police car waited on the road. They sent me to St. Joseph Hospital Psychiatric ward. I was confused and out of my mind. I even thought that they wanted to kill me. A few years passed. Once I went to Police 14 Division, a police officer told me that he was the police who rescued me from Lake Ontario. He said that he did not swim to me and save me because he cannot swim at all. He praised me that I could swim back by myself. I did not feel funny. They knew I was on the break wall. They sent a police officer who could not swim to save me. They did not care about me at all! I was not sane at that moment. My life was hanging by a thread.

Everything has passed and I am stable now. I have friends and my own house that my late husband left to me. I can enjoy the scenery on the lakeshore. I wish that all the disabled people have a good place to live and do not commit suicide.

44

Ben

Ben is a personal support worker. Most of his clients are rich old women. Why did he choose this job? The reasons should be told at the beginning.

Ben was a timid boy. He studied in school silently; most his classmates even did not notice him. Yet boys were boys. Some bad bullies did not forget him. They beat him or destroyed his books and stationery. He was afraid to go to school. He did not tell his father either. He did report it to the vice principal, but after 2 or 3 months, the bad boys bullied him again. He began to play truant and his school marks were low. After he graduated from college. He began to seek a career. His major was social work. He hoped that he could work at the school and help students just like him. He did not find a chance to be a social worker. He was depressed. Ben is a nice looking lad. A woman who is over 40 likes him and hires him to be a secretary. In the daytime, she is the boss. At night, he accompanies her. He felt that his life suddenly becomes easy. It lasts three years. Finally, his father found out the truth. He beat Ben badly and not just once. It was very painful and he used his hand to hide his butt. His father roared "If your butt is itchy, scratch it." He obeyed his father and scratched his butt. He knew that he committed a big mistake. He quit this job and tried to find another job. He really did not know what kind of job he could do. His father suggested that since you like to service old women, you had better to be a personal support worker. If you want to repeat the same mistakes, you let me know and I will cane you. He is shy and goes back to school to finish the personal support worker certificate. The job's opportunities are many. He soon is hired by a private long term care centre. He works hard and many clients like him. Some clients introduce him to their friends who need help. Ben has stable income and more chances to choose clients. Some seduces come. Some old women like him, and offer higher money for services. Ben never forgot that his father taught his a lesion and what he said to Ben. He did not follow the clients' offers. He did his own duties cleanly. Sometimes, he felt that it is hard to refuse. He stands in the corner and scratches his butt. His father does not beat him. Yet he said to his son I trust you. Ben's tears dropped. He knew that good behavior wins respect and trust.

45

Elisa

Elisa is a social worker who works in the Reconnect Community Health Services. ***Reconnect Community Health Services*** *is a not-for-profit health service organization located in the west end of Toronto that provides services. www. torontocentralhealthline.ca*

I am a client here. I like the social workers, nurses, and many employees there. They help us solve the problems and make us happy. Yet Elisa is exceptional. She is a trouble maker. Everything that she did is not helpful but makes things worse than before. She is an invisible minority. Now she is my social worker. When we talk together, she always makes me very upset. Every time she delivers medicine; she asks me some questions. She never carefully listens to what I say. she repeats or asks me the same questions all the time. No matter in the winter or summer, she stays in the car and calls me to meet her outside the door. I wait over 5 minutes to see her. I never experience this situation from other people. Many employees from Reconnect call me outside my door. Sometimes, I sleep on the second floor. I need time to go downstairs and see them. They never compliant and treat me well. Elisa purposely forgets important things. Once, after visiting me, she suddenly, called me and lied to me: "Government workers want to go to your house to fix your basement water leaking for free." I felt very happy and moved. Soon, one day, two people came to my house, one with badge. They went to my basement and check it carefully. They finally said that there was no mold. I asked did you fix the water leaking. They said no. Elisa makes me feel disgusted. Today, she went to my home. just like before, she called me and let me wait outside for over 5 minutes. She asked how is my dog BUDDY; I said that he is in the doggy training school. She purposely asked what is the name of the school. I did not tell her. she said that she wanted to talk to them. I was scared. I do not trust her at all. She is not kind hearted to me.

Not just me, many clients in Reconnect did not like her at all. We all hope that one day, she will be fired. It is fair for us.

46

Special Halloween

Today is Halloween. Because of COVID-19, the government warned people to not go out for candies. At the beginning of October, the government said that they would not cancel Halloween this year. I bought 100 Nestle chocolates for kids. But last week the government changed the rules, I ate them all. The TV news informed us that the Nights of Lights on northern Keele Street had over 1 million lights in the square. People can drive by and watch them. The tickets are from $ 35 to $ 65. Visitors must drive a car to avoid cross infection. Since I have no car, I just can stay at home.

At 5:00 pm, I sat outside my house to watch the children. On our street, only a few houses are decorated. Soon a group of kids and some adults passed me. A boy with York Regional Police costumes, a police stick and a fake gun drove a 2 wheeled scooter passed me. I was very curious. I asked him why he did not wear a Toronto Police costume. He said that this uniform is a real one. A York Regional policeman gave his uniform to him. I like it very much. That boy was very funny, he pointed his fake gun at his own head; I laughed at him. He recognized and shot me many times. Another two kids wear bugs' customs, and one boy had donkey clothes. I feel that it is the funniest one. Some parents wear costumes too. My neighbour's twin girls came home. They held a Halloween party yesterday in their grandma's backyard. One wears a cat's outfit, the other wears a rat's outfit. No kids knocked on the doors like last year. Some homes put candies, cookies, and chips outside the houses, so the children could get them. I saw two girls one with clown's mask, the other had a clown face drawn on her face and wore a clown's wig. They were very cute.

I sat outside for over 1 hour; I decided to follow the kids to see our neighbourhood. Just one block away, there was kids' heaven. Almost every house had decorations. I saw a bear's costume, which makes me recall that my schoolmates gave me the nickname big bear. I asked the mother of that "bear" "May I take a photo with him?" She talked to the "bear"; the bear agreed. She took a picture for us. She told me that the "bear" is a girl. I was surprised. Some house owners drank beers outside. They put candies in small plastic bags, paper bags and boxes. Many tables have hands' sanitizer on. I cannot avoid the temptations and begin to collect the food.

Outside it was very cold. I went home. I counted what I got, totally 10 bags. This year I did not give away candies but grab some for myself. It is special for me as an adult. I hope that next year it will be normal so more kids can go out for Halloween.

47

Church

I joined the Church of Jesus Christ of Latter Day Saints in 2005. I experienced life changes. At the beginning, I did not know anybody. I even did not have time to read the Book of Mormon since I studied at school. My first husband was an active member in our church. My late husband joined the church under my support. He and I enjoyed the church members' care and love. My late husband always said that he felt very happy and comfortable in our church. After he passed away, we sealed in heaven in our church's Temple.

I love our church. Here I learned how to treat people. To know right from wrong. I did not confuse them anymore. I also made friends in our church. When I was wrong or not quite sure, I talked to our bishops and learned from other church members. When I was sick in hospital, church members visited me and brought food to me. I knew our beliefs: poverty, chastity and obedience, although they are hard to follow. When I was young, I had a bad temper. I often fought with others. I seldom got love from others except for my father, who sometimes also beat me. In my mind, churches are bigger than schools. I could say that I grew up in the church.

Now it is near Christmas. Just like before, I bought many boxes of chocolate for my church friends. The Macneils are over seventy years old. They look after me just like I am their niece. I gave them 2 boxes of chocolate, because once, Mr. Macneil joked that he fought with his wife over the chocolates. After he said that, we all laughed. This year, Mrs. Macneil gave me an envelope, I opened it. It was a Christmas card and 20 dollars. I called them and wanted to give back their money. They were very serious and said that this was not for the chocolate; they wish that I would be happy for Christmas. I was deeply moved. I called my father who is in China and told him this story. He was moved too. One of my family's teachers from church Jie Wong, always says that she is my godmother. She often makes phone calls to me. She helps me find my boyfriend. Sometimes, she visits me and brings delicious food to me. This year she brought half Sauce Duck to me. It was very tasty; I ate up in one day. The other of my family's teachers is a role model for me. She always cooks food for our church's banquets. She always brings a lot of food and drink for us.

I was born and grew up in China. When I came to Canada, I was twenty six years old. In China, I went to churches for curiosity. Here, I believe in God. I knew my plan of salvation. Compared with society, churches are the earthly home of God. I am God's daughter, and I am blessed by Him. One day my late husband and I will live with our heavenly Father forever.

48

Buddy in the Private Training School

My fur ball son (puppy) Buddy went to dog training school on September 13th, 2020. This is a boarding school. The trainer let me bring smoking bones, treats and daily dog food. I spent over $ 200 to buy them. I called a TAXI and 4 neighbours came to my door to help me. Buddy became the centre of my community. When the TAXI came to the school, the trainer helped me to take the dog's food to the school. He lets me say goodbye to Buddy, and send him to the backyard. I signed the contract then went home. I miss him very much. In the mean time I can also totally clean my house and enjoy my leisure time.

Today nine weeks has past. I went to school to learn how to train Buddy and to bring him home. I came to the training school very early so as to wait outside the school for 2 hours. The trainer made a DVD about how to teach Buddy and his achievements. I watched the DVD first. I learned to give orders to Buddy such as down, sit, come, stay, out, and take it. These look easy, but when you say that, it is pretty hard, for the dog to do it exactly. In the DVD, Buddy is an obedient boy. He follows the trainer's orders. He was greeting the guests, learning to drop chicken bones, and how to cooperate with people to have a bath. My weakest part is to walk Buddy. The trainer shot the video for walking Buddy on some busy streets. Buddy did not fight with other dogs anymore. He also did not try to escape. He followed the trainer very well. The coach teaches me how to control the leash, how to use my body to help Buddy behave, and how to punish him too. He taught me that if Buddy does not obey, use your hand to pat his nose, and do not give him treats. If Buddy dose not walk well, we stop walking and let him sit a while, or use our feet to kick his paws. The coach taught me the most important skill to walk a dog is that let the dog walk beside or behind me. The dog will believe that you are the boss, otherwise he will do everything that he wants to do and even hurt you very much by biting you hard. I need to train him at home first, then I walk him outside. He said that my dog is super hyper, so avoid letting pedestrians pat him while you are walking him.

Buddy loves to play with other dogs, because he is a big bully. He bites other dogs hard and tries to make love with girl dogs. He is tall and strong, so he seldom fears other dogs. The coach taught me that if Buddy bullies other dogs hard, I should say: "Buddy stay!" and call him to come back to me. "Buddy come!"

I felt happy and paid the tuitions to the trainer. I took the TTC home. When Buddy came to our home, he immediately fought with my cat. They ran from the first floor to the second floor and back again. He is really a big bully! I called him "come"; he ignored it. He even stole my food on the dining table. I wanted to punish him, but I had not seen him over 2 months. I love him, so I did not do it. He did not rip my pillows anymore. I am very happy, because he broke my 9 pillows. I almost had no pillows at all. He also did not bite me hard either. He once bit my ankle so that it bled. My arms were all black and blue, and were swelling all the time.

Today, I brought one box of chocolate to the trainer. He was very happy. This training school is a family school. The father and three sons opened this school. Their father taught me a lot of knowledge about how to handle a dog. For example, using your heart to give orders to your dog. Say orders sharply. Do not always talk to them too much. They will be too excited or lose interest etc. I like the school. I will cherish this memory and DVD forever.

49

Dennis My Late Husband

Security Anecdotes

Dennis had done the security job for twenty five years. He often talked about it. He worked for the Nestle Canada Ltd.

Once, when he went to the company, he heard that somebody had dumped 47 tires in the company's basement. Somebody heard about it and even went there to see whether some tires can be matched or not. Another interesting thing was that a man dumped the construction garbage in the basement when Dennis passed through the parking lot. He felt very upset and called Rushed (another security) to stop him. Rushed was very angry and almost jumped through the roof.

As the largest food processing factory, securities main duty was to stop employees stealing food. Employee theft prevention was a high priority. One day a man left his underwear in his locker, since the factory was too hot. But when he finished the job, he found that somebody had taken his underwear! What a mess!

Family

Dennis' grandfather was a shoemaker. He was so poor that he had no tools. Every time he needed to borrow some tools to make shoes. But he was a very good skilled worker. Dennis' father was a cleaner. He worked until he was seventy two years old. He could renovate houses. He fixed up his house as well. When the Eaton Centre manager saw the brilliant results, he wanted to hire Dennis' father.

His father did not accept the offer. From Dennis' mother side of the family, his uncle was a judge. When the judge passed away, police protected the funeral car to the grave yard. Dennis went to the funeral and never forgot about it.

I miss him

Dennis passed away five years. Every day, I lay in the bed that we slept in. I cannot sleep well. I recall that he told me of his experiences with humor and wit when we laid in bed. I even miss his snoring. He was very optimistic. He used his big sense of humor to illustrate his opinions and ideas. When he was diagnosed in cancer, he was not afraid. He consoled me often. He liked to buy books. We have over one thousands of books, although he did not read that much. In our home, every bedroom and dining room has bookshelves. Now I see these books on the shelves, I feel satisfied. I love my late husband. He treated me like his daughter. He led me, guided me and walked beside me, no matter whether the things were big or small. He knew that I like food, so he often treated me in restaurants. I buried him near his parents. (50 meters from their tomb) It is very expensive, yet that is his wish. I as his only wife, I should do it for him. When I die, I will be buried with him. I love you Dennis.

50

My Birthday

Today is my real birthday November 23rd. I celebrate it with my 2 best friends. One is a Turkish lady; one is my accountant Mervyn. Outside it is snowing heavily. The Turkish friend woke up at 8:30 AM and cooked the lamb pumpkin pockets. She is very smart. She can cook many kinds of Chinese and Turkish foods, which are very clean and delicious. I love her cooked food. She studied in Beijing China for three years. She said that she loves China and Chinese food.

The Turkish lady drove a disability wheel car. She came to my home which was not that easy. Some the TTC subway stations do not have elevators for people with disabilities. I had waited at the bus stop near my home over half an hour. She came. I was deeply moved. In this kind of bad weather, she still came and celebrated my birthday. When we came to my home, I called Mervyn to come. Soon all three of us began to eat. I did not buy a birthday cake this year, since my puppy wasted a lot of my money. I am short of money now. Mervyn likes Chinese food too, although he is a white Canadian. She cooked a whole big pot of the lamb pumpkin pockets. We just ate one third of them, then the three of us all felt full. Mervyn was excited and talked a lot. I was a little bit sleepy. We gave my puppy Buddy a lamb pumpkin pocket. He liked it and ate it up fast. The Turkish lady gave me a real pearl necklace as my birthday gift. I cherish it. I am so lucky! I can spend my birthday with my friends in Canada. I immigrated to Canada over eighteen years ago. I experienced spending my birthday alone; in mental illness hospitals, or in a shelter. I am satisfied with my life now. After eating, I gave her 65 dollars for the fillings of the lamb pumpkin pockets and said thank you to her.

I asked Mervyn to revise my essay. He did it carefully. I was happy to finish my second book on my birthday. It is the best birthday gift I am giving to myself ever.

In the evening, I called my father who is in China and told him my birthday events. He was very happy too. He praised me to continue studying and writing. He wished that he could see the new book soon.

Printed in the United States
By Bookmasters